Bethlehem

by Octavio Solis

A Samuel French Acting Edition

New York Hollywood London Toronto

SAMUELFRENCH.COM

ISBN 978-0-573-69822-4 Printed in U.S.A. #29259

MUSIC USE NOTE

Licensees are solely responsible for obtaining formal written permission from copyright owners to use copyrighted music in the performance of this play and are strongly cautioned to do so. If no such permission is obtained by the licensee, then the licensee must use only original music that the licensee owns and controls. Licensees are solely responsible and liable for all music clearances and shall indemnify the copyright owners of the play and their licensing agent, Samuel French, Inc., against any costs, expenses, losses and liabilities arising from the use of music by licensees.

IMPORTANT BILLING AND CREDIT REQUIREMENTS

All producers of *BETHLEHEM* *must* give credit to the Author of the Play in all programs distributed in connection with performances of the Play, and in all instances in which the title of the Play appears for the purposes of advertising, publicizing or otherwise exploiting the Play and/ or a production. The name of the Author *must* appear on a separate line on which no other name appears, immediately following the title and *must* appear in size of type not less than fifty percent of the size of the title type.

In addition the following credit *must* be given in all programs and publicity information distributed in association with this piece:

***BETHLEHEM* was originally commissioned by American Conservatory Theatre, San Francisco, California. The world premiere was produced by Campo Santo and Intersection for the Arts**

BETHLEHEM was first produced by the Campo Santo + Intersection in San Francisco, California on July 10, 2003. The performance was directed by Octavio Solis, with sets by James Faerron, costumes by Jocelyn Leiser, lighting by Jim Cave, properties by Katherine Covell, and sound by Drew Yerys. The production stage manager was Nancy Mancias. The cast was as follows:

MRS. DEWEY . . . . Margo Hall
LEE ROSENBLUM . . . . Sean San Jose
MRS. BUENAVENTURA . . . . Catherine Castellanos
MATEO BUENAVENTURA . . . . Luis Saguar
DRU . . . . Marcelina WIllis
SHANNON/SONIA . . . . Anna Maria Luera

CHARACTERS

LEE ROSENBLUM (LEANDRO GUERRA)

MATEO BUENAVENTURA

MRS. BUENAVENTURA (AMA)

MRS. MIRANDA DEWEY

DRU

SHANNON TRIMBLE

SONIA

BARRY'S VOICE

MEDICAL EXAMINER

SHANNON and **SONIA** are played by the same actor. The part of the **MEDICAL EXAMINER** can be played by **DRU** or a disembodied recorded voice. **BARRY**'s voice should be recorded using the voice of the actor playing **MATEO**.

SETTING

The play takes place in El Paso: Mateo's backyard patio and front yard. Lee's motel room.

The action flows smoothly from one location to the other, and from one time to the other.

TIME

The time is the present.

ACT 1

(Against the desert mountain background of West Texas, in an old El Paso neighborhood, the sun rises on the Buenaventura house. **MRS. DEWEY**, *a stern woman of middle age, enters mournfully singing a gospel tune as she carries a suitcase marked with crosses and handwritten scripture. She kneels before the house and opens the suitcase, revealing an ornate shrine to her young daughter. She takes her Bible out and erupts in a shouted prayer.)*

MRS. DEWEY. Come, oh Lord. Come forcibly here, come irresistible to my side, impel the fury, rouse it from its shell and impel yourself in it; pay it back, this crime dipped in God's blood; send my darkened angel to impel the justice from hell's own drum and strike this world down strike this world down strike this world down for me!

*(***LEE**, *in his mid-20s, wearing requisite Dockers and sports coat, appears silhouetted in the dim light of early morning. He carries a small recorder in one hand and a small white paper bag in the other. Severely jet-lagged.)*

LEE. Cool southwest Texas morning mist. Crisp blue desert peaks behind me. El Paso ready to go into dog heat. I am right on the cusp between past and past.

MRS. DEWEY. Strike all time and place for me, Lord!

LEE. I don't believe in premonitions because they never amount to much. But I feel like this story is meant for me.

MRS. DEWEY. And send me your Wingéd Wrath!

LEE. It is, after all, my first story.

MRS. DEWEY. Are you him? Are you my angel?

LEE. Angel? Me?

MRS. DEWEY. Are you not summoned?

LEE. Ma'am, I'm Jewish. But can I ask what you're doing out here?

MRS. DEWEY. Go away.

LEE. Are you praying for him? Ma'am, are you praying for Mateo Buenaventura?

MRS. DEWEY. Don't say his name to me! You don't know the demon!

LEE. I read the pertinent facts on the plane.

MRS. DEWEY. Then you know him even less!

LEE. Tell me, then.

MRS. DEWEY. I know what he did to her. I know what he did to her pertinent facts. He came upon her innocence and thrust his hand in and pulled out – .

(She thrusts her hand inside his coat and takes his wallet out.)

LEE. Hey!

(She takes his driver's license out, examines the back facing, and throws it back to him.)

MRS. DEWEY. You haven't signed. Still in possession of your organs if not your wits. Hallelujah, thank you, Jesus.

*(**LEE** grabs his wallet back. **AMA**, an old woman with old world ways, a steel bun on her head, steps out with a broom toward **MRS. DEWEY**.)*

AMA. You again! GET OFF! Get off my yard!

MRS. DEWEY. There is no truth in his mouth, his eyes are pits for vipers –

AMA. He's done nothing to you! Nothing! Leave us alone!

MRS. DEWEY. His mouth is a wide open grave, his tongue seduces –

AMA. Get away from us! SHOO! *¡ANDALE, VIEJA CABRONA! ¡MALDICION!*

MRS. DEWEY. YOU ARE MALEDICTION! YOU BESHAT HIM INTO THIS WORLD!

AMA. ¡YA!

(She drives **MRS. DEWEY** *away.)*

MRS. DEWEY. *(as she runs off)* God shall avenge, oh yes, hallelujah, Lord! etc…

LEE. Are you Mrs. Buenventura?

AMA. He won't see you.

LEE. Ma'am. If I could take a moment to explain –

AMA. He won't see nobody.

LEE. Is that what he says or what you say?

AMA. Don't be so smart with me. I know what you are. The grass dies where you stand.

LEE. *(handing her his card)* Lee Rosenblum. This is our magazine.

AMA. *(spitting on it and tossing it aside)* Smut.

LEE. Ma'am, please. I think you and your son deserve a fair hearing –

AMA. Get off!

(She swipes him with her broom on the face. Bread spills out of the bag all over the ground.)

LEE. Ow! Fuck!

AMA. Idiot! You shouldna ducked! I was gonna miss you anyways!

LEE. My tooth.

AMA. Don't be faking. I'll know if you're faking. Good grief.

LEE. Jesus, I only brought some sweet bread.

AMA. Good grief almighty.

LEE. God, I'm bleeding…

(A man appears in the back. Shrouded in shadow. He is more shape than substance.)

MATEO. Ama.

AMA. I told him.

MATEO. Did you hurt him, Ama?

LEE. Mateo?

AMA. I was trying to scare him off.

LEE. Sir, could I have a glass of water, please? And some tissue.

MATEO. Get him in the house.

AMA. He's a liar and a weasel.

MATEO. Pick up his bread and get him in the house right now.

(The man edges away. **AMA** *helps* **LEE** *pick up the bread and they go inside as* **MRS. DEWEY** *steps forward and picks up the calling card.)*

MRS. DEWEY. Already blood on the front steps. Blessed are the wise, blessed are the true, the upright and innocent, but woe to him who bleeds at the Devil's door.

(The shady arbor of the backyard patio rises out of the background. Old Mexican tile on the ground, wrought iron furniture, and stone benches. **LEE** *enters across from an ominous-looking terra cotta figure of some Aztec deity.)*

LEE. A dark entry into a darker living room and then she leads me to this patio. Ice pack for the swelling. My Rockports on his turf. Small pre-Columbian ceramic figurine, looking at me like I'm Cortez. Too late. You lost.

*(***AMA** *enters with a cup of herbal tea.)*

AMA. Here.

LEE. What is it?

AMA. *Yerba buena* to dull the pain. But I ain't sorry, in case you're thinking.

LEE. Who's the holy roller?

AMA. Don't pay her no mind. Damn freak. *Esta loca.* When *mijo* came after his release, there was a whole group of people making a *mitote.* Saying get him out, he'll murder our children and what-not. Neighbors who used to say hello, spitting in my face. And the news people. Lotsa cameras and trucks *y que nada.* Seeing my house on TV, hearing the news lady call me names. But two weeks pass and look: only her. Regular as the sun.

LEE. She's sure mad about something.

AMA. Mateo won't discuss her. So don't.

(She goes. **MATEO** *enters, unseen, eating the sweet bread.* **LEE** *glances again at the ceramic figurine, almost touches it.)*

MATEO. *Pan sagrado para la pena del diablo.*

LEE. Excuse me?

MATEO. My old man used to go out and get bread for us when I was a *chavo.* His way of making peace.

*(***MATEO** *offers him a piece.* **LEE** *takes it.)*

How's your jaw?

LEE. I'll live.

MATEO. My mother, *sabes,* gets overprotective sometimes.

LEE. She packs a good swing.

MATEO. Her house is the only place on earth I'm welcome.

LEE. Am I?

MATEO. Depends. How much you know about me?

LEE. Not nearly enough. Mostly stuff about the "incident". Court papers, news clippings. A little about your odd jobs, fleabags, drinking binges. Nobody really knows you.

MATEO. Is that you're after, Mr. Rosenblum? The Mateo no-one knows?

LEE. If you'll let me. We want to do an in-depth for the magazine. A couple hours a day for a couple days. Get to know you, your life, your version of things. Larsen, my editor, would offer remuneration but it's not our policy.

MATEO. I don't care about no damn money. I wanna be left alone. I'm not what they think, you know. I was innocent of that crime.

LEE. Then say it for me. Let me do a spread on you and show people your side of things. A real human, with feelings and memories, more than a criminal act and a news story, but more like us, like real *gente,* Mateo.

MATEO. Real what?

LEE. People. Real people.

(He approaches **LEE.***)*

MATEO. Are you Mexican?

LEE. Me? No…I….

MATEO. Waitaminnit.

(With his finger, **MATEO** *delicately pulls down the skin under his eye.)*

MATEO. I look in your eye. That red tomato edge in your eye and it look Mexican to me. It got that shredded Mexican pride in it still. Overripe. Sore to the touch. Sleepless. The pride that never sleeps, but waits. Waits for something just outa reach of this world. Your clothes are a mask. Your name is a mask. That makes you white. But what makes you Mexican like me is your soul itself is a mask.

LEE. I'm Lee Rosenblum.

MATEO. That's what your card says.

LEE. I'm from New York.

MATEO. Your complexion is from New York.

LEE. Look, am I doing this story?

MATEO. Tell me your given name. *Tu nombre santo.* Or no interview.

LEE. I told you my name.

*(***MATEO** *gives* **LEE** *something in a hanky and goes. The patio recedes into the background as* **MRS. DEWEY** *steps forward on the front yard.)*

MRS. DEWEY. Look what's come from the belly of the beast. What's he given you, Mr. Rosenblum?

LEE. My tooth.

MRS. DEWEY. Will you give him good press and put him on your cover? Make him a household name? Scant consolation to the people he's hurt. None at all for Shannon Trimble.

LEE. Who are you? What's with this vigil? Are you related to Shannon?

MRS. DEWEY. What do you care? You only come to know the devil. Not his victims. Whore yourself, do your spread.

LEE. There's no spread. I'm not doing it.

MRS. DEWEY. Too late, Mr. Rosenblum. The Beast has struck his deal with you. Hallelujah.

(She goes, singing to herself, as an austere seedy motel room emerges. There's a bed and a nightstand. **LEE** *violently opens his briefcase, spilling all over the bed photos of the crime scene.)*

LEE. He doesn't know me. He doesn't know me. He doesn't know me. He doesn't know me. He doesn't know me. Fuck him. He's doesn't know shit about me! I don't need this fucking interview.

(He takes a quart of bourbon from his brief and almost downs a swig when he realizes something about the room. He takes it in.)

Motel room. Twin sized bed. 19" TV. Remote screwed into the table. My eyes screwed to the grisly pictures of high school death. Blood on the carpet. Smears on the drapes. A twin bed soaked in gore.

(He picks up one of the photos on the bed.)

Tell me, Shannon Trimble. Do I need this story?

*(***SHANNON***, a pretty Texas teen, sultry and a little drunk, slinks in from the shadows.)*

SHANNON. Does the story need you?

LEE. Intelligent, pretty, all of 17.

SHANNON. I got me ID that says 21.

LEE. Popular at school, especially with the boys.

SHANNON. But I like mine with experience.

LEE. A penchant for older college guys, some even older.

(The deep brutish voice of **BARRY**, *bellows from off:)*

BARRY. *(off)* SHANNON!

SHANNON. SHADDUP, BUTTHOLE! *(to* **LEE***)* Barry's such a goon.

LEE. What do I do, Shannon? I can't lose this spread.

SHANNON. Watch that hootch, big guy. I might want me a shot later.

LEE. I walk away now and blow my first assignment and Larsen won't like it. He'll never give me a better one.

SHANNON. I need a dollar for the juke box.

LEE. That lady thinks I don't care about you. I do. If I believed in God, I'd want to know what the hell He was thinking letting someone as young as you end up on a coroner's slab.

SHANNON. Mister, God ain't got nothin' to do with it. Desire bereft of body, that midnight car with the headlights off, and all the darkness to spare…

(He starts to follow **SHANNON** *as she drifts away. A blinding flash out of the darkness.* **DRU** *enters with a camera. A worldly-wise photographer, she moves like the world is her studio.)*

LEE. Dru!

DRU. Howdy, Rosenblum.

LEE. What are you doing here? I thought you were in Israel or wherever.

DRU. Well, somebody's gotta bust your balls. Can I have a whiff of your breath freshener?

LEE. Let me get you a glass.

DRU. *(tossing him a small film roll container)* Here.

*(***LEE** *pours her some.)*

LEE. Jesus, it's good to see you. When did you get in?

DRU. Just this afternoon. Is this the best you could do? Motel 666?

LEE. I was looking for something that would approximate the place she died in.

DRU. Method Journalism. Up yours. *(drinks)*

LEE. How the hell did you find me?

DRU. Larsen. He thought it'd be a real laugh to pair us up again. *(seeing the photos on the bed)* Whoa. Jesus. He really filleted her, didn't he?

LEE. Don't look at them. They'll give you nightmares.

DRU. I've seen worse. I got first-hand experience with monsters all over this planet.

LEE. Dru, seriously. What are you doing here? Because –

DRU. Relax, I'm here to take his picture. You should be grateful. I'm the one who got you this job, remember.

LEE. It's just that, you know, stuff between us –

DRU. I learn my lessons. I'm actually over you, Rosenblum. And I'm engaged.

LEE. Really?

DRU. No. Ha! But I could be. I got friends in the press corps, you know.

LEE. I don't doubt it.

DRU. So tell me about this creep. How soon can I set up a shoot?

LEE. It's not happening.

DRU. Wait a minute, wait a minute, hold the phone.

LEE. I'm not doing it. The fucker started playing head games with me and I just said no way.

DRU. What kinda head games?

LEE. Riding me for information, turning talk around to me, getting personal.

DRU. Is that it?

LEE. I do a serious interview, Dru. I don't involve my personal life.

DRU. What serious interview? Jesus, you work for a nudie magazine. And personal life, give me a break. You never sit still long enough to have one. Six months in bed with you and all I got to know was your bed.

LEE. I have a rule about professional distance.

DRU. *(aiming the camera at him)* Me too. It's called depth of field.

LEE. Dru...

DRU. *(advancing toward him)* We never really officially broke up. Technically we're still in the game. As a journalistic team, I mean.

LEE. You're saying I should do this.

DRU. Only way to get the close-up is to get up close.

LEE. Something about him, though. He gets you in this space. He takes the doors and windows out.

DRU. I'll keep mine open for you then. Rm 216. I better go unpack. I want to be ready for this perv.

LEE. Let me soften him up. In the meantime, I got someone else you should check out.

(Lights change. **MRS. DEWEY** *enters.* **DRU** *takes out her camera and snaps away as* **LEE** *recedes with the motel room.)*

MRS. DEWEY. O Lord, praised be your name, I pray for deliverance from trouble and fear! –

DRU. Great! Do that again!

MRS. DEWEY. My King and my God, the wicked will perish as you so command –

DRU. Arms in the air, eyes to God!

MRS. DEWEY. Providence shall make it so.

DRU. That's it!

MRS. DEWEY. Providence shall see it done.

DRU. Good!

*(**MRS. DEWEY** stops and turns her steely gaze to **DRU**.)*

MRS. DEWEY. The Word is made Flesh and the Flesh shall be commanded home.

*(**MRS. DEWEY** takes her charm and places it around **DRU**'s neck. She goes. **DRU** follows her as **AMA** appears with **LEE** in the patio.)*

AMA. *¿Otra vez?*

LEE. Tell him…Leandro is here.

*(***MATEO** *enters.)*

MATEO. Leandro who.

LEE. Leandro Guerra. I was born in Fabens, just a few miles from here.

MATEO. Bring Leandro some *horchata,* Ama.

*(***AMA** *goes.)*

You've had *horchata,* no?

LEE. Do we have a deal?

MATEO. How the hell did you end up a Rosenblum?

LEE. My parents split up. Mom took me to New York and remarried. She died within the year and my stepdad raised me.

MATEO. That's some trick. Tradin' off skins just like that. Didn't yer old man have a say in it?

LEE. I don't know. He disappeared into Mexico with my little…

MATEO. Yeah?

LEE. Listen, all the credentials you need are in this folder.

MATEO. Shit on your credentials. I'll never talk to a Jew reporter.

*(***LEE** *moves to take up his folder.* **MATEO** *places his hand over it.)*

MATEO. But I *will* talk with a Mexican.

(They smile at each other and **LEE** *prepares his tape player.)*

LEE. You and your Mom seem pretty close.

MATEO. Nobody closer. Greatest woman I ever known. Ain't nothin' in the world I wouldn't do for her.

LEE. Buenaventura Tape One. Nine am.

MATEO. Do I need to talk loud or what?

LEE. Don't worry. This'll pick you up. So she's a great cook, huh?

MATEO. The old country way. None of this microwave stuff. She uses old cast-iron *ollas* handed down from her *nana.* She gets everything from the market in Juarez.

(**AMA** *returns with a tray of food, horchata and whiskey.)*

MATEO. *¿Que no, Ama?*

AMA. Try it. *Sabe rico.*

LEE. Mmm. This is good.

AMA. Put some *chile de arbol.* Better when it's spicy.

MATEO. One of the delicacies I missed in the ward.

AMA. *Sopa de lengua.*

MATEO. Tongue.

LEE. Thanks. Really good.

(**AMA** *plants a kiss on his forehead and goes.)*

MATEO. She's made me this *caldo* since I was a little boy. My dreams swirl in this soup.

LEE. Before we start…can I ask you?…Who's the woman out there?

(**MATEO** *drops his spoon into his bowl and glowers at* **LEE.***)*

MATEO. Do I have to answer for every little pissant bitch on this earth? Am I to explain the logic of idiots? *Esa pinche vieja es una puta! PUTA!* I ain't been allowed to live my own life. I ain't been alone in the presence of a woman other than my mother in more'n TWELVE years! You know what that does to a man? People like that make me wish I was back in the psyche-ward.

LEE. So you don't know who she is…

MATEO. No. *(He enunciates into his recorder.)* Fuck No.

LEE. Did the treatment help?

MATEO. *(taking his whiskey)* Oh yeah, big help. I'm a rehab wonder. My personality disorder's diagnosed, addressed, and redressed. I'm a fully medicated citizen.

LEE. You sound bitter.

MATEO. It wasn't my idea to declare me loony-tunes. That was my lawyers.

LEE. You didn't want the insanity plea?

MATEO. The whole shebang made no sense to me, but damn if the jury didn't buy it. Suckers'll believe anything. I got drawer fulls of bullshit medication I'm supposed to be taking. *(***MATEO** *raises his glass.)* This is all the sedation I need. Wild Turkey! No way am I sick and no way did I touch that girl.

LEE. I may have my facts wrong, but didn't your semen place you in the room?

MATEO. I don't deny some consensual messin' around. I just don't recall when or how or what.

LEE. You blanked out.

MATEO. Blinded by the Turkey. Slipped in the gap. The interstice, doctors called it.

LEE. Are you an alcoholic?

MATEO. Uh-uh.

LEE. Do you have nightmares?

MATEO. No.

LEE. Did you ever torture cats, dogs?

MATEO. Never.

LEE. Into self-mutilation?

MATEO. No.

LEE. What about compulsive masturbation?

MATEO. Get outa here!

LEE. Enuresis?

MATEO. Oh for cryin' Jesus!

LEE. What about your father?

MATEO. What about him?

LEE. Well, I read that he was in and out a lot. Always on the move. But there's no mention in the trial transcripts of any past abuse.

MATEO. I like that word. Abuse. Good fucking clinical word.

LEE. Did he whup ass on you?

MATEO. He applied discipline.

LEE. I can guess how severe that was.

MATEO. Well…guess.

*(**LEE** pauses as he is taken aback by the reversal.)*

LEE. He slapped you around some. Knocked a few teeth out. Whipped your bare ass with the buckle end of the belt.

MATEO. Colorful.

LEE. Left you bleeding on the floor sometimes. Without food. Your mom probably tried to stop it, but a man's home is his dungeon. And yours is his buckle. Am I right?

MATEO. And the buckle?

LEE. Something with his name probably. Big and silver and…cold.

MATEO. You guess pretty good.

LEE. Did he mess with you in other ways? *(**MATEO** snorts.)* What's so funny? If you don't want to tell me, cool. If you can't remember, I'm cool with that too. But sometimes, Mateo, after discipline, there's a need to comfort, a need to love again.

MATEO. Seein' him undo that buckle could only mean one of two things and I hated both of them.

LEE. Did he do these things in Spanish or in English?

MATEO. What the hell difference does it make?

LEE. What if his beating words were English and his loving words were Spanish. 'cause what does a boy understand, and what stays in his head as strange language? Words of another world raping you all your fucking life.

MATEO. How do you know my shit so well? Are all our old men so alike?

*(**LEE** hesitates for a moment.)*

LEE. My father was a man with a grudge. He resented having to live in a country that resented him. He was one of those large impenetrable men who walked around like they're in a bullring.

MATEO. Yeah.

LEE. On nights after he'd spray my sheets with discipline, I'd get up, inch slowly down the hall, cross the long line between me and my baby sister's room. Crawl in her bed and stay there all night.

MATEO. Watching for him?

LEE. Lying beside her, counting out the little embroidered roses on her pillowcase. You're not getting her, I kept saying.

MATEO. You saved her.

LEE. I wish. He ran off to Mexico with her. Haven't heard a word since. I've never told anyone. That I remember it at all is.... (**LEE** *shuts off the tape player.)* I'm supposed to be asking the questions.

MATEO. Can I ask you one more? What's that word, enuresis?

LEE. Bedwetting.

MATEO. That one I did! I pissed them sheets till I was fifteen.

*(**MATEO** bursts out laughing as he goes. The motel room appears with **SHANNON** waiting by the bed, dressed in the white smock of a forensic psychiatrist with a stack of files.)*

SHANNON. *(throwing files on the floor as she speaks)* On more than one occasion, he was able to subvert the process of analysis to his ends.

LEE. No shit.

SHANNON. He likes the company of other patients but only insofar as they serve his needs.

LEE. Why does he make me talk about myself like that? My sister and all that...

SHANNON. He suffers from a superiority complex. He cannot tolerate those who think him inadequate, antisocial, or unclean. So he levels the psychological playing field.

LEE. He can't be that cunning. He's a lowlife.

SHANNON. A mendacious individual who blurs the lines between conjecture and fact, truth and insinuation.

LEE. Why is he even talking to me?

SHANNON. He likes the attention. In all my years on the ward, I never saw anyone so enjoy his incarceration and treatment.

LEE. He thinks he's innocent.

*(**DRU** enters distractedly, her gaze caught on something off.)*

DRU. Lee…

SHANNON. Exculpation through denial. Denial of his crime, denial of his past, denial of his denial.

*(**BARRY'S VOICE** bellows from off.)*

BARRY. *(off)* SHANNON!!!

SHANNON. Later, sugar.

*(**SHANNON** rushes off into the shadows. **DRU** turns.)*

LEE. I'm going to have to play hardball with you, sir.

DRU. Lee.

LEE. Hey.

DRU. You okay?

LEE. I think we're getting somewhere. He gave me *sopa de lengua.*

DRU. What's that?

LEE. Tongue.

DRU. Gross.

LEE. I'm going to transcribe the interview off the tape.

DRU. I can do it for you if you want.

LEE. No, it's fine. I'll do it. *(He notices her agitation.)* Are you okay?

DRU. You told me to see that lady on the vigil. So I did.

LEE. What happened?

DRU. Well…you know, I watched her pray and sing Jesus to herself for a while and got a few good shots. Then just like that, she gave me this charm, blew her candle out, and locked herself in her van. I left a note with my phone number saying I needed her to sign a release and then came back to my room to jump in the shower and when I came out…

*(**MRS. DEWEY** appears standing by the bed. **LEE** watches the exchange.)*

MRS. DEWEY. Miss Dru? Is that your name?

DRU. How did you get in?

MRS. DEWEY. I came to sign that form.

DRU. Yes. Let me get that for you.

MRS. DEWEY. I'm sorry I was in such a state. When I have the Holy Spirit, all the world is a blur to me.

DRU. You were fine. *(reading her name on the form)* Mrs. Dewey.

MRS. DEWEY. Your friend seems fascinated with the butcher. He's not interested in anything I have to say.

DRU. He's always been a little self-absorbed.

MRS. DEWEY. You, on the other hand, pretend to understand my situation.

DRU. I understand you're in some kind of pain. You act like you're the mother of the girl he killed but they moved to Canada years ago. So who are you?

MRS. DEWEY. Some years ago, the Lord called my daughter Chelsea home. She was in a freak automobile accident. For two weeks, she remained in a coma and my husband and I prayed for her deliverance. When she was declared brain dead, sweet Christ spoke to me to let her go. So I had the plug pulled on my baby. The heart was removed, shipped to a hospital in Dallas, and transplanted –

DRU. I'm sorry about that, but what does that have to do…

MRS. DEWEY. …transplanted into Mateo Buenaventura.

DRU. Oh…. my god.

MRS. DEWEY. My Chelsea saved that man. He had an obligation to live well and serve others and stand as an example of God's grace. He received a miracle, a gift, a second chance at life, and what did he do just months after receiving my daughter's organ? Murdered a girl exactly her age. The soul of my Chelsea in him and he commits this butchery. How can she rest as long as a part of her lives in that monster? He entered into a covenant with God and he shat all over it! They said in court that it was her heart that made him crazy! He blamed my Chelsea for the murder! So I sit in front of his house every day to remind him that he's living on my daughter's time.

DRU. What for? What good can it do her now?

(**MRS. DEWEY** *places her hand against* **DRU***'s chest.)*

MRS. DEWEY. Whose heart beats here, Miss Dru? Do you know that every heartbeat has its own signature? God forbid you should come that close, but if you do, listen to that demon's heart and see if don't you hear my Chelsea calling. Crying to be rid of that filthy man.

DRU. What do you want from me?

MRS. DEWEY. Don't take his picture. Mateo's an unholy and dangerous man and he knows his time is nigh.

DRU. Nigh?

MRS. DEWEY. God is my surgeon, Miss Dru.

(She goes. **LEE** *reads the name on the form.)*

LEE. Miranda Dewey. That's why she checked my donor status.

DRU. My heart is still pounding.

LEE. Come here.

DRU. I'm getting a double-lock on that door, I swear…

(**LEE** *draws her close.)*

DRU. *(cont.)* I pride myself on knowing my subjects. I tell myself this is what I do. But what my camera knows and what I know are not the same. They're not the same.

LEE. Do you want to spend the night here?

DRU. Just tonight. Just…you know…

(She kisses him, tentatively. As he speaks, **LEE** *holds* **DRU***, then guides her toward the bed. She unbuttons her blouse and lies on it facing him.)*

LEE. I tell myself we're just trying to ward off this encroaching darkness. But something else is happening. She feels good. Warm. She lets me feel things I haven't allowed myself in a long time. Both of us, we're lonely as hell and we count on each other's detachment, but this evening, we make real love and lie in each other's arms desperately feigning sleep, filled with this vague sense of shame.

(He takes a large canvas bag from under the bed and the room recedes. **MATEO** *enters, bringing with him his patio.)*

MATEO. Guilt and agitation. I bring out the best in people. I wouldn't worry. This shame grows into this wonderful fucked-up thing we call conscience.

LEE. Did you pick that up in the psyche-ward?

MATEO. No, I learned that in church. So she wants pictures of me?

LEE. Just a couple shots. Candid. Dru wouldn't take but twenty minutes. She'll improve on those old prison mugs everyone's seen.

MATEO. I'm not sure a chick in my house is a good idea right now.

LEE. She's not a chick, she's the best in the biz. She'll capture your essence.

MATEO. Is that what you got in the bag? Some essence?

*(***AMA** *enters with a plate of food.)*

AMA. *Mijo, aqui te traigo tantita comida para que no te canses.*

MATEO. *Ay, Ama. Mira.* You did all this today?

AMA. *Andale, a comer, mijito.*

MATEO. *Gracias.*

(She kisses him tenderly on the forehead and goes, casting a malevolent eye on **LEE**.*)*

MATEO. *Ama* never had a chance to be good at nothing in her life but being *Ama.* But what's an only son for?

*(***LEE** *unzips the bag and takes out some 8x10's, which he lays before* **MATEO**.*)*

LEE. I think you know Shannon Trimble.

MATEO. Sweet Jesus.

LEE. Let's see: deep purplish contusions along the neck area, bruising on the hands and wrists, numerous violent hacks to the torso, a deep vertical gash one centimeter left of the sternum, with the heart violently taken out of its chamber.

MATEO. Please take them away.

LEE. Trauma throughout.

MATEO. I don't doubt it. I hope the poor girl died quick.

LEE. The poor girl's name is –

MATEO. I know her name! I seen the pictures! And I'm sorry, that was Evil, an altar for pure Evil, that poor body was not a body but a sacrament to hell!

LEE. When the maid found her, all her teen spirit had soaked the mattress. How's your lunch?

MATEO. Fine.

LEE. They never found her heart. Not a trace. Where'd you put it?

MATEO. Nowhere. I had nothin' to do with nothin'.

*(***LEE** *takes tools from the bag. Cutting shears. A small hatchet. A crude boxcutter. He ceremonially sets them on the ground before him.)*

LEE. Prima facie.

MATEO. God almighty.

LEE. Evidence rendered at first view.

MATEO. Where did you get those?

LEE. The hatchet and the boxcutter came from a woodworking shop. The cutting shears I bought at a hardware store. They're not the actual weapons you used but they never found those, either.

MATEO. *Madre Santa.*

LEE. Talismans of death, Mateo. These are for the science of pain.

*(**MATEO** feels the tools with a mixture of awe and terror. He recalls.)*

MATEO. I was at *Los Tres Aces* drinking myself blue. Exchanging slurs with other drunks and losers. Trying to make the words out in those Patsy Cline songs on the jukebox. Funny how all the petty grievances you got with life just swarm all over you when you're fucked up on Wild Turkey. You think if you keep perfectly still hunched over the bar, they'll ignore you and overrun the poor slob in the Ryder cap next to you. But no. They smell the booze and the self-pity and press theirselves on you like nobody's business. So I left. I got in my pickup and drove.

LEE. Where to?

MATEO. I just drove. The last I recall was me trying to put the broken knob back on the radio. Next thing I know it's six in the morning and I'm standing naked on the shallow end of this icy pond off the Interstate. Shakin' all over like the palsy. The rest is public record.

LEE. You don't remember the hatchet? Or the other tools?

MATEO. I kept them in the toolbox in the bed of my truck. But I didn't use them, and toolbox got stole.

LEE. Shannon had had a fight with her boyfriend. She forced him to pull over and she jumped out of his car. Some truckers remembered seeing her bearing north just a mile from her parent's house.

(From the surrounding dark, **SHANNON** *strolls drunkenly on and stands in her own space.)*

MATEO. It's always that close.

LEE. Did you see her, Mateo?

MATEO. No.

LEE. While you were reeling in the cab of your truck grumbling about the shitty hand life dealt you and the radio fulla static and the little knob in your hand, did you look up and see this beautiful young thing on the roadside?

*(***MATEO** *slowly turns and sees her standing in the cold.)*

MATEO. Maybe I pulled over.

LEE. I woulda. I woulda eased to the shoulder and lowered the window on her side and said:

MATEO. Can I get you out of this cold, miss?

SHANNON. No thanks.

LEE. I wouldna taken no for an answer.

SHANNON. Why not?

MATEO. 'cause, hell, I got some good dope in here that I don't know if I want to smoke all by myself.

SHANNON. I'm almost home, anyways. I should go on.

MATEO. I'll drive you to your boyfriend's and we'll all get high. We'll party up.

SHANNON. I don't think he wants me around right now.

MATEO. Whut? You mean he let you walk all alone at this time a night?

SHANNON. Kinda.

MATEO. Well, hell with him. C'mon. I'll take you home.

(She sits next to **MATEO***.)*

LEE. Wasn't that the way it happened?

MATEO. What was her name?

SHANNON. Shannon.

MATEO. Are you as potted as I think you are, Shannon?

SHANNON. No, not really. Hey, that's my house you just passed.

LEE. Where did you take her, Mateo?

MATEO. Let's not go home right away. I'm really in need a company.

SHANNON. But I really have to get home.

MATEO. I'm really in need of some company, Shannon.

SHANNON. But I'm about to pee.

LEE. Did you take her to your motel room? Is that where you went?

MATEO. Right through that door. I'll get my stash and papers.

(They enter the motel room. **SHANNON** *sprawls on the bed and watches.)*

LEE. While she went to the bathroom, did you go out to your truck? Did you get the tools? What grabbed at you so tightly that you had to use a hatchet to make it let go?

MATEO. I wasn't hardly there.

LEE. What did it feel like? Did it feel like the devil, Mateo?

MATEO. I was driving. Patsy Cline in my head. I fall to pieces. Road all pitch black and the headlights ahead making me blind. I was blind….!

LEE. Look at her, Mateo.

*(***MATEO** *turns to* **SHANNON***, smiling blithely at him. He studies her.)*

MATEO. I'm looking for traces of him on you. For signs of his correction. Did he beat you? Did he whup you with plastic conduit too? Did he run his filthy mouth along the curve of your shoulder and the arc of your neck and the inside of your thigh? Like fathers do.

LEE. Who are you talking to? Is this Shannon Trimble?

MATEO. I'll take you away if you want. I know how he is. Will you come with me?

LEE. Who is this, Mateo?

SHANNON. *(turning to* **LEE***)* Desire bereft of body.

MATEO. Nobody.

LEE. What does your old man have to do with her?

MATEO. Nothing. Shannon Trimble is nothing.

SHANNON. So where's this awesome dope?

MATEO. None of this happened. This is all in your head!

SHANNON. I could use a big ol' doobie to settle my stomach.

LEE. Tell me, Mateo!

SHANNON. Hey, hold on. Are you…are you crying?

LEE. MATEO!

*(***MATEO** *roars with rage and charges the girl. He stops. The hatchet suspended. He turns and plants the handle of the hatchet in* **LEE***'s hand.)*

MATEO. You do it.

*(***LEE** *looks at* **SHANNON***, who sits up and smiles.)*

MATEO. Look in her face. If you can't ruin that, then I never did!

*(***SHANNON** *stands and collects the tools and the 8x10s.)*

SHANNON. Local Girl Found Murdered! Grisly Discovery in Motel Room! Drifter Arrested in Downey Slaying! Brutal Murder Shocks Residents!

*(***SHANNON** *takes the hatchet from* **LEE***.)*

Murder Weapon Found on Writer. Slain Girl's Smile Haunts Journalist. Search for Missing Heart Continues.

*(***SHANNON** *goes.)*

MATEO. I loved her.

*(***MATEO** *goes. Lights change as* **LEE** *speaks into his recorder.)*

LEE. All day restless all day trying to make sense of things see past the face of Shannon see that other face the face that loves him back not Shannon someone else inside her calling him to his evil. Who. Who. All day asking who till the sun peels back the sky to show me night.

(The motel room. **DRU** *is lying on the bed, asleep.)*

LEE. *(cont.)* The motel. Dru in bed. Her own mystery.

*(***DRU** *lifts her head, in the spell of some dream. Her eyes open.)*

DRU. I hear it.

LEE. What.

DRU. In my sleep. The heart.

LEE. Whose heart.

DRU. The girl.

LEE. In Mateo.

DRU. Beating against his chest. Beating to get out.

LEE. Does it get out?

DRU. He's lying on the roof of his house. Flat on his back. Naked.

LEE. His chest bared.

DRU. And it comes out. I see the Dewey lady with the Ginsu knife carve open his chest and pull it out.

LEE. Her daughter's heart. The Dewey heart.

DRU. No. No. Not her heart. Not his heart. Mine. I'm lying on my back looking at my own heart. Oh my God. Oh my God. LEE!

*(***LEE** *shakes her and she wakes with a start.)*

LEE. It's a dream. A nightmare. None of it's real.

DRU. I still hear it beating.

LEE. It's nothing. The ceiling fan.

DRU. What's wrong with me?

LEE. Nothing. Listen. Do you remember the times we went out, the movies we saw, the talks we had in bed with the light out? Do you remember that?

DRU. Sure I do. Don't you?

LEE. Hardly. I remember it mostly like the details of someone else's life, but not mine. I remember wishing I could say I loved you.

DRU. You didn't. But you didn't have to. That wasn't the game.

LEE. I need you tonight, Dru. I can't be alone.

*(**LEE** kisses her.)*

DRU. Why are we here, Rosenblum?

LEE. To get the story.

DRU. Fuck that. Maybe we're the story.

LEE. I mean his story.

DRU. Then get it. I want to go home. Don't you want to go home?

*(Crossfade to **MATEO**'s house. **MATEO** enters with a tray carrying a bottle and a pair of shot glasses.)*

MATEO. Hell, we all want to go home.

LEE. What is it?

MATEO. Mescal. Some tribes in Mexico used it for the visions it produced. *Un tragito.*

*(**LEE** reluctantly takes a glass. They raise the shots and then down them.)*

I didn't make much hay with the other inmates in the Ward. Kept to myself, resisted friendship with the doctors 'cause what are they really after, am I right? These mornings, lately, I been getting up earlier than usual and moping around the house, waiting for you to come. You make me see things, now maybe I return the favor.

LEE. What do you want me to see?

*(**MATEO** pauses for a moment. **LEE** turns on the tape.)*

MATEO. Hot summers stealing pomegranates from the neighbor's yard as a kid. Riding my old bike around the school. Cotton fields thick enough to hide in. Can you see them?

LEE. Acres of them. And Mexican accordions crackling out of some old radio somewhere. Those dangling clumps of red *chiles* on the porch…

MATEO. *(as he pours another set of shots) Ristras.*

LEE. And sitting at the window in Yosemite Sam pajamas watching the dust devils outside.

(They down the next round.)

MATEO. There's a cigar box under my bed filled with mementos, little matchbox car, a couple marbles, a picture of my mom, and this crystal from Carlsbad Caverns...

LEE. I remember Carlsbad Caverns. We all went to Carlsbad Caverns. We all peed in Carlsbad Caverns.

MATEO. *(as he pours another set)* Oh hell, sure we did, after all the Fanta Orange Cola we drank on the way, what'd ya expect?

LEE. Here's to pissin' in the Cavern!

LEE/MATEO. Pissing in the Cavern!

(They toast and drink and laugh awhile. **MATEO** *pours another set.)*

MATEO. Different generations, you and me, but the things we did in this town don't change.

LEE. I wonder how I ended up the way I am. How quickly those dust devils swept me up and took me east. If I'd stayed here, chances are I'd probably live out the pattern of my old man's life.

*(***LEE** *pours another round.)*

MATEO. *Watchale.* You gettin' to the worm.

LEE. It's just like sushi, man. *(They drink.)* You know, in love you can't harbor secrets, you can't hold anything back, not if it's real, not if you really expect to share your lives. That's what love is, and I don't know if I ever knew that, but this girl, she doesn't give up...I could be messing up her life while she makes me feel a little like....shit....what was I saying?

MATEO. That a little love justifies the blazes of hell.

LEE. That's not what I was saying.

MATEO. It's what you meant. You ain't the only one with a sister gone.

LEE. Wait. Wait. You? *(***MATEO** *shakes his head.)* You have a sister, Mateo?

(**MATEO** *gets up to make sure they're alone.)*

MATEO. My mother doesn't know.

LEE. What are you talking about?

MATEO. Keep your voice down! My father had another woman, *en Mexico.* He was gone for weeks, nobody knew where. If Ama asked, he answered her with silence. But one day I said to myself…

LEE. Follow the fucker.

MATEO. We can't talk anymore about this. *No mas.*

LEE. Mateo, you have to tell me –

MATEO. My mother, goddammit!

LEE. You mention that you got a half-sister living in Mexico for the first time, it's not in any of the court transcripts, it's not mentioned anywhere!

MATEO. It ain't relevant!

LEE. I want to get to the truth, Mateo, but you gotta help me.

(A dare is exchanged. **LEE** *drinks the worm. A threshold is crossed.)*

MATEO. Belen. I stole me a car and followed him across the border. To a dusty pueblo called Belen.

LEE. And you saw her.

MATEO. The other woman was older, poorer. But he seemed to treat her better than he treated my mom.

LEE. And he had a daughter.

MATEO. *Toda mi pinche vida,* I felt her presence. In everything I did, a craving for someone. On those rough nights, sitting in my room alone, I used to imagine holding her. My secret sister.

(**SONIA** *steps into the light carrying a large bundle. A young dark beautiful girl of 16 with black hair, dressed in a simple cotton dress. She sets her bundle down, unwraps it and starts to display various folk dresses on the sacking.* **LEE** *does not see her.)*

LEE. She was living under the same roof with that bastard, wasn't she?

MATEO. Over the next couple weeks, I made some trips down. I studied her. The more I watched her, the more I learned about myself. Innocence, love, shit beaten out of me long ago. Unbearable, yes, but it was hope. Only now…

LEE. He was there.

MATEO. Only a matter of time. I had to get her away.

LEE. So you went to her. You told her who you were.

MATEO. No…It was she who came to me.

SONIA. *(hardly looking up to see them) Oye joven. ¿Que haces aqui en el sol? Ya te apareces como un Hershey.*

(**LEE** *turns and sees her.)*

LEE. Oh my god…

SONIA. *¿Sabes lo que te digo?*

MATEO. Like you, I was struck dumb.

SONIA. What's the matter? You want me to talk English?

MATEO. She's waiting.

(**LEE** *slowly walks toward her and he is transported to an ancient village plaza, blazing with sun. He seems younger in this space.)*

LEE. Yes.

SONIA. Okay. Why you wanna look like a Hershey? Move to the shade. There's lots of shade in Belen.

MATEO. I freeze up with a kind of terror I never felt before.

LEE. I like it here. I wanna get browner.

SONIA. *Americano.* What are you doing?

LEE. What do you mean?

SONIA. I seen you. Sitting in the car across the street. Walking around the *Ayuntamiento. La tienda.* Sitting here in the *zócalo.* Like a Hershey.

LEE. So?

SONIA. So you're spying on me.

LEE. I'm not spying on you.

SONIA. Then what are you doing in Belen?

LEE. What do I say?

MATEO. You're waiting for a friend.

SONIA. Who's this friend?

LEE. No-one you know. He's coming up from *la Capital* and we're going to take off to California.

SONIA. Big Hershey lies. Help me with these.

*(**LEE** helps her unpack and spread across the floor several long beautiful skirts of brilliant colors. Lacey frills. Colorful folk embroidery.)*

SONIA. Right about now all the *turistas* are suppose to come out of the *mesónes* into the square. To buy their colorful *curios* and gifts to take back across. Look around. You see any *turistas*?

LEE. No.

SONIA. I see one.

MATEO. Look at the dresses, fool.

LEE. They're beautiful.

SONIA. *Ama y yo,* we make them in our house. The fabric comes from Jalisco but the embroidery is all ours. The lace here. I did that.

LEE. It's very nice.

SONIA. All by hand. Those little purple roses are not easy.

LEE. Have you been doing this for a long time?

SONIA. Long enough. Just sewing for one night is a long time.

LEE. Do you have one of your own?

SONIA. Me? What good is a dress like this to me? Where am I going to go wearing these *rositas*? It's very poor in this *pueblo, chavo.* I don't want to look haughty.

LEE. I think you'd look like a princess.

SONIA. Okay. Who are you? Why are you following me?

LEE. My name is…Mateo. I'm from El Paso. I didn't mean to scare you.

SONIA. I'm not scared. It's just been a while since a boy took any notice. In so obvious a way, I mean.

LEE. Was I obvious?

SONIA. *¡Chale!* Sometimes it's like I don't even have to look up. I can feel your eyes all over me. I catch myself doing things. Like stretching in front of the window. Wearing my good shoes to the store. Stealing Ama's make-up.

*(**LEE** looks down in embarrassment.)*

SONIA. The way these tourists haggle. I better lower prices to half.

(She turns the sign around. Price cut to half.)

MATEO. Sitting in the sun, with the mockingbirds' squawk above the empty square and a few bees drunk on nectar buzzing over the dresses, I form a word out of the urge to cry.

LEE. Sonia.

SONIA. How do you know my name?

MATEO. How?…

LEE. Sonia, do you miss having someone to share secrets with? Someone you don't even have to talk, you know he feels what you feel –

MATEO. He senses things inside you –

LEE. – he lives that other part of you.

SONIA. I don't know if I understand…

LEE. Look. One dress is so different from the other. The sleeves are different –

MATEO. – the embroidery –

LEE. – the patterns. But they share the same material.

MATEO. The same fabric. –

LEE. – They breathe the same.

SONIA. They do.

LEE. I breathe the same. You and I. The same air. Am I wrong? Don't you feel it?

SONIA. Like this?

(She kisses him.)

LEE. No. No. Sonia. No.

SONIA. *¿Que pasa? ¿Que no te gustó?*

LEE. Yes, I liked it but…

MATEO. This is what evil means.

*(***LEE*** walks away, leaving her alone with her dresses, still in the memory.)*

LEE. You feel like a traitor to your own best cause. All your itinerant heroism turns to shit. You like it. You like her tongue in your mouth. You realize all along, this girl you're stalking, you're compromising her soul.

MATEO. I wasn't stalking her. *(to* **SONIA***)* Was I?

*(***SONIA*** gathers her wares and vanishes into the blackness.* **AMA** *returns.)*

Wasn't I just following little roses on a dress?

AMA. I have the water running in the bath.

(He goes. **AMA** *gives* **LEE** *a look. He is still in a daze.)*

AMA. Call before you come over. He sleeps in on Wednesdays.

LEE. *Sra.* Buenaventura, would you be open to some questions? Off the record?

AMA. Mateo says nothing we say is off the record. So nothing we say.

(They exchange a look and she goes. **MRS. DEWEY** *appears on the front lawn.)*

MRS. DEWEY. Here he comes. The left hand of death. What excuse does the monster give you now, Mr. Rosenblum?

LEE. Stay away from my photographer, Mrs. Dewey.

*(***LEE*** moves on.)*

MRS. DEWEY. You feel compassion for him already, don't you? Don't you?

LEE. You don't know him. You don't know anything but your own pain. His story is deeper than your pain.

MRS. DEWEY. Will you follow it then? Will you follow the deed to its bed of straw, its first breath, its suckle of human blood? Will you draw from the same swollen tit?

LEE. The days of gods and devils are long gone, Mrs. Dewey. And you're beginning to realize that. Or your prayers might have been answered by now.

*(**LEE** goes. **MRS. DEWEY** cries after him.)*

MRS. DEWEY. He'll answer them! He will! But He moves according to his own time! Isn't that right, Lord! Ain't it so, Father! *(singing) He Keeps his Promises!.... (She stops and then lets the doubts wash over her.)* Why dost thou stand afar off? Why dost thou hide thyself in my time of trouble? Answer me, Lord...speak to me, Lord....

(She goes in a cloud of doubt. The motel room. ***DRU*** *enters.)*

DRU. Lee?

(She sees the laptop near the bed. She opens it and turns it on. She starts up the program on the computer. ***LEE*** *enters, startling her.)*

LEE. What are you doing?

DRU. I was hoping to read what you've written so far –

LEE. Turn it off.

DRU. C'mon, I need to know what angle you're taking on him.

LEE. Sorry, Dru. That material is confidential, between me and him, no-one else.

(He shuts the laptop off and tucks it under the bed.)

DRU. Are you forgetting this confidential material is going in a magazine?

LEE. I don't care what happens after I turn it in. Till then, hands off.

DRU. What is it with you?

LEE. I told you, Dru. Professional distance. I think I need some time by myself tonight, okay?

DRU. Jesus, Lee –

LEE. No, Dru, I'm sorry. We can't do this.

DRU. What's going on?

LEE. I need my key back.

DRU. Why are you being like this? This isn't you.

(no response)

It's him, isn't it? What's he telling you? What are you telling him? Oh no. You haven't told him about us, have you? Have you?

LEE. I know what I'm doing.

DRU. I'm not so sure.

LEE. He's just a story, Dru. The key.

DRU. *(tossing him the key)* Fuck! I'm still getting my shoot.

*(***DRU*** turns and starts setting lighting equipment, tripods, etc. in* **MATEO***'s house as* **SHANNON** *enters, taking out some bloodied pictures.)*

SHANNON. Here's pictures of me and my brothers that we took at Ruidoso. Snow all around and them laughing. That's Sal. And big brother Brent trying on his new skis. My daddy never smiles 'cause of his teeth. But Momma always looks like a movie star. And here's me. Making a snow angel.

(She shows a photo of her reddened corpse sprawled on a white sheet.)

BARRY. *(off)* SHANNON!!!

*(***SHANNON*** goes.* **DRU** *checks her equipment.* **LEE** *preps his recorder.)*

LEE. Remember, do what you normally do, let me handle the chitchat, play it cool and he'll be cool.

DRU. I know what I'm doing, too, Rosenblum.

*(***DRU*** plugs in a cord. Lights come on.)*

LEE. Dru…last night I wasn't myself, I was –

DRU. Forget it. Just let's get this done so I can beat the hell out of here.

*(***MATEO** *enters with his glass of whiskey.)*

LEE. *Mateo, buenos dias.* This is the shooter I told you about. Ms. Suffolk.

(As **MATEO** *turns to see her, she snaps a Polaroid of him.)*

DRU. Call me Dru. Hope you don't mind all this gear.

MATEO. *(eyeing her warily)* No, I don't mind…

DRU. Promise, I won't break anything. Give me a minute to get all plugged in.

LEE. The way this thing'll go is you sit there and we'll talk like usual, and she'll work around us. Just be natural, she'll find the best shots.

MATEO. *Está bien.*

*(***MATEO** *sits.)*

LEE. Is something on your mind?

MATEO. No.

LEE. Are you sure? What's up?

MATEO. Nothing.

(Lights flood the area, forcing **MATEO** *to cover his face.)*

DRU. Sorry!

MATEO. Do we really need all these lights?

DRU. Won't know till I get a light reading.

LEE. Your eyes will get used to it. Just relax. I need my recorder.

(He goes and whispers to **DRU** *as* **MATEO** *uncomfortably takes his seat.)*

LEE. Jesus Christ, Dru. What the hell are you doing?

DRU. You don't hear it? That beating?

LEE. Hear what? What are you talking about?

DRU. Forget it. Just stay outa my way.

MATEO. Is something the matter?

LEE. No. Buenaventura Tape Fourteen. Nine am. Photo session. Testing, testing…

MATEO. She seems tense.

LEE. She's not. She's a pro.

*(**DRU** comes right up to him with a light meter.)*

DRU. Shit. I'm barely getting a reading. Can you move your hand, sir?

*(**MATEO** lowers the hand from his face.)*

You eat up a lotta light, Mr. Buenaventura.

(She adjusts a lamp and takes another reading.)

LEE. So what do you want people to think when they read this article about you?

MATEO. They can think what they like.

LEE. What if they still think you're guilty of that crime?

MATEO. Then you haven't done your job.

*(**DRU** starts snapping **MATEO** with her Nikon.)*

DRU. Don't mind me.

LEE. This is what we mean by candid. This is how she works. Right, Dru?

DRU. Move out of the frame, Rosenblum.

*(**DRU** proceeds to snap a series.)*

MATEO. Does she have to get that close?

LEE. Dru?

DRU. Nice.

MATEO. I ain't accustomed to people being in my face.

DRU. Eyes here. Chin up. Good. Good.

MATEO. Especially members of the opposing sex.

DRU. Don't move. Excellent. Nice. Good.

MATEO. Are we done?

LEE. I think we're done.

DRU. Wait. One more thing. May we unbutton the shirt?

MATEO. My shirt?

DRU. Right. Could we open it up, please?

MATEO. What for.

LEE. Dru, is this appropriate?

DRU. I got a little more left on the roll. If we could just get the shirt open. Please.

MATEO. You didn't mention this.

LEE. You don't have to do it.

*(**MATEO** unbuttons his shirt. A long ugly scar down the middle of his chest is exposed.)*

DRU. Like that. Like that. Hold it open. Beautiful.

(She starts snapping.)

MATEO. You like this?

DRU. Yes sir. It's lovely.

MATEO. A real sight to behold?

DRU. Oh yeah, really something.

MATEO. You want me to touch it? You want me to lay my hand on it?

DRU. Sure.

(He does. She continues snapping away.)

LEE. I think that's enough, Dru.

MATEO. I got this from an operation.

DRU. Yes, I know.

MATEO. A heart transplant.

DRU. I know.

LEE. Dru, back off.

MATEO. I got a young lady's ticker inside me.

DRU. Uh-huh.

MATEO. Sometimes it talks to me, you know? It does. It says things.

DRU. I bet it does.

LEE. Stop it.

MATEO. It's saying something now. You wanna know what it's saying?

DRU. What is it saying?

MATEO. It's sayin'…. *(suddenly grabbing **DRU** by the throat.)* MAKE SURE YOUR FACE IS THE LAST GODDAMN THING THIS BITCH EVER SEES!

LEE. MATEO! NO!

MATEO. FUCKING CAMERA! FUCKING BITCH WITH HER FUCKING LIGHTS!

DRU. Okay…

LEE. Let her go…

MATEO. *¡Ya me cansé de tus pendejadas, pinchi puta cabrona!*

(He turns her camera toward her face and snaps the shutter.)

LEE. Okay, Mateo! Cut the bullshit, okay, okay?

(He releases her. **DRU** *sinks to the floor, gagging and gasping for air.)*

MATEO. Photo session over. Get this cow out of my house.

*(***MATEO*** rips the cords out of the wall. The lights go out.* **DRU** *gets up. As she goes, she turns and aims her camera.)*

DRU. Hey, asshole.

*(***MATEO*** turns. She snaps one and staggers out. He starts after her in a fury then turns to* **LEE***.)*

MATEO. What is this! Did you tell that cunt about my operation!

LEE. I'm sorry, okay! Jesus! Calm down!

MATEO. What was that damn thing she kept putting against me? Was that some radar thing or what?

LEE. It's a light meter! She needs it for her f-stops.

MATEO. What the hell are f-stops?

LEE. F-stops are…. shit, I don't know! It has to do with the camera!

MATEO. We're done. Give me that tape.

*(***LEE*** hands over the tape from his deck.)*

This heart was given me fair and square. If you think I ain't thankful, you're wrong. But it's my life now. I don't owe a thing to nobody.

LEE. Mrs. Dewey think you're evidence of the Devil.

MATEO. Dewey out there can KISS MY HAIRY BROWN ASS! YOU WANT IT, LADY, YOU WANT IT BACK, GO AHEAD, TAKE IT!

*(**MATEO** rips off his shirt, baring his scar to the world.)*

MATEO. RIP IT OUT OF MY FUCKING CHEST! I DON'T GIVE A SHIT! THINK I NEED YOUR GODDAMN CHARITY TO LIVE, THINK AGAIN! TAKE BACK THE DAMN HEART AND GET THE HELL OFF MY BACK! PUSSY, THAT'S WHAT YOU ARE! A PUSSY!

*(**MATEO** falls to his knees in exhaustion. **LEE** keeps still.)*

MATEO. I don't know about the Devil, but I got evidence of God. Coming out of the operation, I saw my ticker in this pan beside me. Really pathetic ruined looking sorta thing. I got this sudden perverted impulse to touch it. Don't know why. Maybe to be sure it was real. I reached across and sank my finger into it. It felt like meat.

LEE. Please. We're close. I can feel her. Sonia.

*(**MATEO** sits up and begins his story. The lights change.)*

MATEO. She waits outside the door of her house at night.

*(**SONIA** enters into the light, cutting a sharp silhouette. She is quietly but ardently searching.)*

MATEO. Looking for me. Standing like a cut-out with the porch light behind her. Three nights in a row, I sit out there under an old mesquite and wonder how that paper doll shape would feel against me. During the day, I sleep in this run-down *Plaza de Toros* closed for the season. But the nights I sit awake watching her, trying desperately to strip away the parts that are not my sister.

*(**SONIA** calls softly for him.)*

SONIA. Mateo...

MATEO. Summons me on the third night.

SONIA. Mateo...

MATEO. She knows I'm there. She knows I will come.

SONIA. Mateo…

*(**LEE** moves irresistibly toward her. She offers an old blanket.)*

SONIA. I brought you this for the cold.

LEE. I'm not cold.

SONIA. We can sit here and talk for a while. They're asleep. *Sientate.*

*(**LEE** spreads the blanket for her and they sit.)*

SONIA. You're a strange boy. You go away but you don't go away.

LEE. Quit calling me boy. I'm older than you think.

SONIA. You feel so familiar. Like I've met you before. Why did you turn away when I kissed you?

LEE. I wasn't expecting it. Girls in Mexico, I heard you move fast.

SONIA. We just like to pick our fruit early.

LEE. What do your parents say about this?

SONIA. *Pos, mi amá es muy estricta.* She thinks I'm too young to see boys. Still, she likes to sit in the *placita* and watch the courting rituals with me.

LEE. What's your father like?

SONIA. He's there. Except when he's not. He works in *Tejas. Apa*'s a very serious man. Always a lot of things on his mind. He drinks.

LEE. How is he…with you?

SONIA. He loves me. In a world of black and white, I'm the only one he sees in color, so he says. He's gone a lot, but every time he comes home, he brings me bolts of fabric from *el Norte.* The best pima cotton. What's your father like?

LEE. Very different. In his world of color, I'm the only black and white.

SONIA. Is he mean to you?

LEE. Mean I prefer to indifferent. My father also goes away for long stretches.

SONIA. Do you know where?

LEE. No.

SONIA. We live such different lives. How can we be so alike?

(They kiss. **SONIA** *rises and takes his hand.)*

LEE. No, Sonia.

SONIA. In your car. No-one will know. What's wrong?

LEE. I want you so much.

SONIA. Is that bad?

LEE. Yes.

SONIA. Then I don't care.

*(***LEE** *rises as* **SONIA** *disappears into the darkness.)*

MATEO. In the back seat of that old car. Stricken with something we thought would kill us. Stuck together like dragonflies.

LEE. Is this it? Is this where it starts?

MATEO. You tell me.

LEE. This is your story, Mateo.

MATEO. You so fuckin' interested, why don't you finish it?

(He drops the tapes in his whiskey glass and goes. **LEE** *slowly retrieves the tape from the whiskey glass and plays it back on his recorder.)*

LEE. Sonia.... *(nothing)* Sonia...

(Silence. Then...on the recorder...)

SONIA'S VOICE. *Aqui....aqui te espero, mi amor...*

LEE. Sonia....

SONIA'S VOICE. *Aqui...*

*(***LEE** *turns and sees her rise out of the dark.)*

SONIA. The same air, you said. Right from each other's lips.

*(***LEE** *goes to her and kisses her.)*

LEE. In me I feel your heart.

SONIA. And yours beats in me.

(They kiss. **MATEO** *appears.* **LEE** *and* **SONIA** *begin making love. Over them, the presence of the masked* **MEDICAL EXAMINER,** *who may be played by* **DRU.** *Over the following sequence,* **SONIA** *slips out of being and* **LEE** *plays out the perverse fantasy alone.)*

MATEO. She's mine. My secret now. I kiss her face.

MEDICAL EXAMINER. Massive swelling of the tongue due to strangulation.

MATEO. I kiss her neck.

MEDICAL EXAMINER. Singular purplish contusions circling the upper neck.

MATEO. I run my tongue like a razor along the seam of her skin.

MEDICAL EXAMINER. Deep incisions from the base of the xiphoid process of the sternum to the base of the neck.

MATEO. I kiss her lovely breasts.

MEDICAL EXAMINER. Lateral incision across the upper chest cavity.

LEE. Oh god….

MATEO. I draw myself inside her.

MEDICAL EXAMINER. Severe damage to the chest plate and rib cage.

MATEO. Tear through the membrane of her sex.

MEDICAL EXAMINER. Massive tearing of the pericardial sac.

LEE. No! Please!

MRS. DEWEY/DRU. Massive blood loss.

MATEO. She is mine!

MEDICAL EXAMINER. Pulmonary artery transected.

LEE. Sonia…!

MATEO. *¡Alma mia!*

MEDICAL EXAMINER. Heart dislodged from abdomen.

SONIA'S VOICE. *¡Leandro!*

*(***LEE** *achieves climax and remains suspended in his ecstasy.)*

MEDICAL EXAMINER. Traces of semen detected in the uterine canal and throughout the vaginal area.

(Lights go to black. A single light reveals **SHANNON**, *her throat blue, her torso a gaping bloody mess. She smiles at* **LEE** *through bloodied teeth.)*

SHANNON. So…where's that doobie you were gonna roll us, lonely boy?

(Tableau. Blackout.)

End Act One

ACT 2

(The arid desert explodes into view. Heat and creosote. **DRU** *enters, gagging fiercely.)*

DRU. Air. Air.

I come out of that house with his hand still on my throat. His fingers sorting through the scraps of my breath, scream, wail, gasp. Fuck.

I toss my guts at the curb. What was I thinking? Why did I fall apart like that?

*(***MRS. DEWEY** *enters and stands apart.)*

DRU. I see her. Seeing me. Giving me this look.

MRS. DEWEY. Like the Rapture's nigh but not for me.

DRU. I should go back and pack my camera and take the first flight back to New York. I should resign this assignment and forget this woman and you and that noxious prick. But I'm groping for air and following her.

MRS. DEWEY. Walking.

DRU. Three shadow-lengths behind.

MRS. DEWEY. Then the bus.

DRU. Which takes us to the farthest stop out of town and into the desert we go and even though she never once looks back –

MRS. DEWEY. You're there.

DRU. We stand in the crazy heat among the sage and creosote. Holding my Nikon like a lung. For what seems like hours. Then…

*(***MRS. DEWEY** *crumbles to her knees and sobs openly.)*

MRS. DEWEY. LIAR! YOU LIAR! Call yourself a just God! But you're nothing but a LIE! YOU LIE!

DRU. Mrs. Dewey…please…

MRS. DEWEY. He told me he would punish that demon! Look at what that monster's done to you! He'll kill you next time!

DRU. I won't let him. Please stop.

MRS. DEWEY. I abjure you! I *renounce* you on this day! *OHH! (collapsing)* My baby…I want my baby back. Chelsea…

*(***DRU** *strips her camera off and rushes to* **MRS. DEWEY,** *who collapses in tear on the ground. They hold each other and weep.)*

DRU. Okay. I'm here…I'm here.

MRS. DEWEY. Chelsea…

DRU. I know, Miranda, I'm very sorry…

MRS. DEWEY. Oh God. How long since I heard that spoke.

DRU. What?

MRS. DEWEY. My name. Miranda. All the things I made forfeit in my life. The man I was married to for twenty years. The Girl Scout cookies every year. The PTA meetings. All gone since Chelsea.

DRU. She must have been really something.

MRS. DEWEY. Oh she was nothing special. Girl wouldn't do her homework, always boys boys boys, and I had to ground her a few times. But that just meant she was in the house laughing. We played with our little dog Patsy that she adored as all get-out. All her children's books piled up in my closet that I was saving for her children. Reading to her at night, kisses on her cheek, night-night rituals of mom and girl.

DRU. God, I wish I'd had someone like you growing up.

MRS. DEWEY. All forfeit now. That life is a mystery to me.

DRU. It's still your life. You have so much to cherish. What do I have? What good is my life? What am I living for? When that animal grabbed my throat, all I could think was I can't die yet. I haven't loved yet. Jesus, I have to fall in love once before I die.

*(***MRS. DEWEY** *rises to her feet.)*

MRS. DEWEY. If you care for Mr. Rosenblum, take him away from here. Mateo is infecting him. You're his only hope. For some of us, the past is past and there's no recourse but wrath.

*(**MRS. DEWEY** leaves.)*

DRU. I turn around and head back to the main road and catch the bus, and sit as it takes the long route home. Every step I take to this motel, I tell myself I won't come to your room. I won't tell you. You won't listen, anyway, right?

*(**LEE** appears in his room.)*

Right?

LEE. I would never have let you do this if I knew you'd be in danger.

DRU. My question to you is what do you plan to do.

LEE. I'm going to finish the interview.

DRU. About us, Lee. What are you going to do about us?

LEE. Jesus, Dru…

DRU. I thought we had a chance. That last night I felt a part of you so brittle, so in need of mercy, you held me like you needed me…

LEE. Oh god, don't. –

DRU. YOU NEEDED ME!…I'm gonna level with you, Rosenblum. At the shoot, I thought it was his heart I was hearing. But it was mine. My heart. I'm really hearing it for the first time.

LEE. I have to work on the story now.

DRU. What story, Lee? What fucking story? I've seen your laptop. There's not a single word written anywhere in there! Just a title.

LEE. You had no right –

DRU. **Mateo Buenaventura**! That's all that you've written! Nothing but his name!

LEE. What do you want from me!

DRU. You! I want you! I want us to fall in love. We're like savages. Living day to day. Eating other people's lives. It's not enough for me anymore. I don't give a shit about the story or the magazine or Larsen! I want to see the real you.

LEE. I'M LEE ROSENBLUM! THAT'S ALL! THERE'S NOTHING INSIDE! NO SECRETS! NO SURPRISES! JUST LEE ROSENBLUM!

DRU. And I'm gone.

*(**DRU** turns to go.)*

LEE. You're leaving?

DRU. The first bird to New York. You want pictures, take them yourself. You wanna stick with this brute, knock yourself out. Frankly, you make a great couple.

LEE. Dru…

*(**DRU** goes.)*

I'll do it myself then.

*(**MRS. DEWEY** enters.)*

MRS. DEWEY. Will you?

LEE. Ma'am, I told you once, please leave my photographer in peace.

MRS. DEWEY. It wasn't me who hurt her.

LEE. Lady, I'm really sorry about your daughter, I'm sorry he had to have her heart to live, and I'm sorry for Shannon Trimble too. But you can't be playing God whenever you feel like it.

MRS. DEWEY. *(taking a large kitchen knife out of her bag)* Not even when God deserts us?

LEE. I'm not getting into this.

(He starts to walk away, then stops and turns.)

Give me the knife.

MRS. DEWEY. Is that why that devil is still alive and my Chelsea dead? Would more faith ever change that? Or is it up to us make things right?

LEE. Hand over the knife, Mrs. Dewey.

MRS. DEWEY. I can't!

LEE. You're not going through with this. Nothing is going to happen to him.

MRS. DEWEY. Why are you protecting him? I don't understand.

LEE. I'm protecting you.

MRS. DEWEY. Listen to your Dru. She loves you. Get away from this man.

LEE. I can't.

MRS. DEWEY. How can you go there? How can you choose him over her?

LEE. Give me the knife, Mrs. Dewey.

MRS. DEWEY. She made me see. She made me see who I was, what I sacrificed to believe in the Lord, in justice and righteousness, and now what? When it all fails, what is there left to believe in?

LEE. Maybe the only thing we believe in is Buenaventura.

*(**LEE** takes the knife from her.)*

MRS. DEWEY. I am in such pain. …

LEE. Go home. I'll take care of him.

*(**MRS. DEWEY** goes, moaning loudly, almost reaching song. **MATEO** enters with his bottle of whiskey.)*

MATEO. A little Turkey? *(**LEE** shakes his head.)* She's pretty agitated out there. Baying like *la llorona.* Gnawing on her tongue. That kinda restlessness breeds murder.

LEE. How would you know?

MATEO. What?

LEE. What do you know about murder? You haven't killed anyone.

MATEO. I've wanted to. Haven't you?

*(**LEE** drops the knife on the table.)*

MATEO. I'm gonna file a restraining order on that cow. How's your lady friend?

LEE. Don't talk about her.

MATEO. I hope I didn't hurt her.

LEE. Don't talk about her.

MATEO. She's a beautiful woman.

LEE. I'm not going to tell you again.

MATEO. What happened? Did you and the purty lady have a falling out?

LEE. It's none of your business.

MATEO. I kinda had a sense about that, you know. I got a nose for that kinda thing.

LEE. What are you talking about?

MATEO. Well, you know, don't you?

LEE. What?

MATEO. You don't know?

LEE. You're fulla shit.

MATEO. You're so goddamn smart, I figured you'da put *dos y dos* together by now.

LEE. What?

MATEO. She loves you.

LEE. You're outa your mind.

MATEO. She loves you but now she's packing her bags and heading off for greener enchiladas.

LEE. You're such a sham, it's incredible.

MATEO. It's all right. It's in the service of our story. I don't know why, I don't know how, but I do believe your Dru is here for a reason. I do believe that, at some cost to her soul and yours, she's gonna get you the cover.

LEE. Where do you come up with this?

MATEO. Where else? Belen.

LEE. What did you do with Sonia? Did you rape her? Did you kill her? Did you cut her open like Shannon Trimble? Did you tell her you were her brother?

MATEO. I hate to bust your chops, but shit's already come down, *carnal.*

LEE. I want to loathe you, Mateo Buenaventura, I want to be morally repulsed by you. But all I feel is pity. I pity your sorry ass. I wish I knew why.

MATEO. Come to Belen. You'll see why. Come.

*(**LEE** resists for a moment, then turns around and calls in desperation.)*

LEE. Sonia! Sonia!

MATEO. Waiting in the bullring. All night. Still musky with sex. Still reeling with love. Sisters are the sweetest fruits.

LEE. SONIA!

*(**SONIA** darts out of the dark into his arms, clasping him tightly. She wears the white dress with the little roses.)*

MATEO. The sweetest.

LEE. Oh god!

SONIA. I'm sorry, I'm sorry! I came as quick as I could!

LEE. I was afraid…I thought something had happened.

SONIA. What? Nothing happens in this *pueblito.*

LEE. What are you wearing? Is this the same one from the *zocalo*?

SONIA. Do you like it? Do I look like a princess? That's what you said.

LEE. Yes.

SONIA. Finally, someone to wear it for.

(They kiss.)

MATEO. Last night I was terrified. I didn't know I could be like that.

SONIA. Me neither. It's like there's this other person that comes out. Who is this? Is this me? Are these my hands? My legs? How do they know what to do? How does that place know how to love?

LEE. It's crazy. I hardly remember what happened. I could have done anything to you and not known. I felt so out of time, so blind. Even after you left, there was this… this –

MATEO. Violence.

SONIA. What do you mean?

LEE. I was losing control, losing myself, it was like being in pain.

MATEO. Causin' it.

SONIA. I would never hurt you, lonely boy.

LEE. What did you call me?

SONIA. Lonely boy.

MATEO. She'd learned that phrase from an American song. Some damn pop tune that poked fun at heartbreak.

LEE. Sonia.

SONIA. Yes.

LEE. I want you to come with me.

SONIA. Come with you? Where?

LEE. Away from this. Back to the States. We can go anywhere. Right now.

SONIA. Now? *¿Estás loco o que?* I can't just take off like that.

MATEO. Don't let her get away!

LEE. Come with me. We'll get you some clothes in El Paso. Hurry.

SONIA. What about *mis papás*?

LEE. Forget them. It's just you and me from now on. *Vente conmígo,* Sonia.

SONIA. I can't. I'm still in school. My mother needs me. My father.

MATEO/LEE. FUCK HIM!

LEE. You don't need that bastard! You don't need to put up with his shit anymore!

SONIA. What are you talking about?

LEE. Poor Sonia. All this time, all those nights, dealing with him. Son of a bitch! He won't get you now.

SONIA. *¿Que dices?*

LEE. I came to save you. Don't you get it? I came to take you away from that fuck. I know what he'll do to you! I know his ways, Sonia!

SONIA. You're crazy!

LEE. He'll come into your room! He'll think he's entitled. You won't be able to stop him! I know!

SONIA. How! How do you come by this filth!

MATEO. Yes. How.

LEE. *Ven,* Sonia. Before he ruins you.

(**LEE** *holds his hand out to her.)*

SONIA. I don't know who you're talking about. My father is good.

LEE. No.

SONIA. He brings me presents and fine pima cotton, he adores me –

LEE. No…

SONIA. I can't. I can't go. *Lo siento.*

(Pause. **MATEO** *calls in a booming voice we recognize as* **BARRY***'s.)*

MATEO. *(as the father) ¡Sonia!*

SONIA. *¡SI, PAPI!*

LEE. I see. I see. You fucking whore. *Puta.* He's already had you.

SONIA. *No lo digas.*

LEE. Go on. Go to him. You want to stay with him, stay with him. GO YOU SLUT!

SONIA. *¡Leandro, no!*

LEE. Jesus, I should have known! You're his *puta,* the *puta* of Belen, La *Puta* Sonia! What a laugh! I come to rescue a whore!

SONIA. Why am I listening to these lies!

LEE. *¡Gracias por todo, Puta de Belen!* Go to that pimp of yours and tell him Leandro Buenaventura appreciates the time with his…the time with his own….

(**LEE** *collapses in tears.)*

SONIA. Who are you?

LEE. *¡VETE! ¡LARGATE DE AQUI! SONIA, POR FAVOR!*

SONIA. *No...Dios Mio....no puede ser...*

LEE. GET FUCKING LOST! BITCH! YOU BITCH! GO BACK TO MY FATHER! LET HIM GIVE IT TO YOU! WHORE!

*(***SONIA** *runs in horror.* **LEE** *collapses, asphyxiated on his own sobs.)*

MATEO. This is it. Where all things rise from, all sin and redemption, all pain and *pinche* delight, this seed, this cradle, this bethlehem, this town in heat. Your black hole. Sucking up the hopes of the sickest most contemptible sonofabitch of all: you.

*(***MATEO** *takes the weeping* **LEE** *into his arms.)*

All the blindness of before, the blank spaces, the check-out times, they were echoes of this, the biggest blank, the lapse in time spent with this little whore!

*(***MATEO** *raises* **LEE***'s face to his.)*

And the gall! The gall of the girl to prefer him to you! You! What you sacrificed! What you exposed! The heart, Sonia, took its disbelief and made it faith for you, for you, sister, lover, whore, devil! You could have saved her, but she went with him and made you nothing! Nothing, boy! The whole time you were with her, you might as well have been with yer old man! You know whut I mean? Do you, Leandro?

LEE. I DO!

MATEO. Before what was in your soul could find its way to her throat, you run. You run to the car, then drive out of Belen, into the desert, it don't matter where.

But she ain't gone, boy. She's here, in this chest, beating like a crazy bell. You want her? You wanna tell her what's really on your mind? If you feel what I feel, and I think you do, you'll go for it. You'll open me up and find her! *Dale, Leandro!* TAKE THE GODDAMN HEART, YOU WORM!

*(***LEE** *charges* **MATEO** *and slams his open hand into his chest repeatedly. Finally, he feels the long ugly scar on*

his chest and kisses it. He collapses in tears as **MATEO** *leaves. Silence as night descends. Then* **MRS. DEWEY** *enters separately, finds a place to set down and open her shrine.)*

MRS. DEWEY. Lord, I offer up this wretched life to you. *(taking a small knife from her shrine)* Make Chelsea see the great sin it is to die this way, but greater yet to live so bitter.

(She places the blade against her throat and tries to slash it, but she cannot. **MATEO** *enters with the duffel bag of tools and starts to cross past her. They see each other.)*

MRS. DEWEY. Devil. *(He pauses, then continues. She stands in his way.)* Devil.

MATEO. Move outa my way, lady.

MRS. DEWEY. I'm not scared of you. Skulking out the back way, like a tapeworm.

MATEO. I done nothing to cross you.

MRS. DEWEY. Like a parasite.

MATEO. Say whatever you want to me. I got rights.

(She spits at him. He takes a step toward her.)

MRS. DEWEY. Come, demon. Come into the light. Oh, yes, thank you, Lord, Praise God.

MATEO. About your child. I'm sorry they put her heart in me. I had no choice in the matter.

MRS. DEWEY. The vilest creature I ever laid eyes on. Viler still close up. The lies gather on the corners of your mouth.

MATEO. I don't mean nobody harm.

MRS. DEWEY. What do you call yourself when you're alone with your conscience? What do the cries of that innocent girl call you at night?

MATEO. You don't unnerstand.

MRS. DEWEY. How is it possible to misunderstand hell?

MATEO. You say I killed a girl. Well, Miss high-and-mighty, you commit your little murders, too.

MRS. DEWEY. Liar.

MATEO. Think about it.

*(**MATEO** reaches into her shrine and grabs a photograph of her daughter.)*

MATEO. Who pulled the plug on your daughter? Who decided she was ready to die?

MRS. DEWEY. FIEND!

MATEO. How much are you responsible? Put it in whatever words you want, it's still the same thing. It ain't like unplugging a table lamp, neither! That was her death.

MRS. DEWEY. Lord Jesus, smite this man.

MATEO. Thass right. Pray, lady.

*(He turns to go as she raises the knife. **MATEO** stops, falls to his knees in pain and calls in another voice.)*

MATEO. Mama…*(She stops.)* Mama, it's me.

MRS. DEWEY. Who…

MATEO. It's me.

MRS. DEWEY. Chelsea…?

MATEO. Mama.

MRS. DEWEY. This…can't be some trick….

MATEO. No, Mama, please. Don't walk away from me. I'm here.

*(**MATEO** comes to his knees.)*

MRS. DEWEY. Child.

MATEO. Remember, Mama, all the things we did together? How we played with Patsy…

MRS. DEWEY. Patsy?

MATEO. Our little dog Patsy. Remember? Remember?

MRS. DEWEY. It's you!

*(She embraces **MATEO** with motherly fondness.)*

MATEO. It's been so lonely, Mama. Being here. Inside.

MRS. DEWEY. Darlin', I'm sorry.

MATEO. Don't worry, Mama. I've felt your closeness all these years, through this skin and gristle, I've felt your love. So true and constant.

*(***MRS. DEWEY*** weeps convulsively.)*

MATEO. Don't cry. I have me a purpose now. I do. In this kinda sleep, the blood of this man passes through me, and you know somethin', Mama? I cleanse it for him, I give it air and light and newness, and I purify him daily, Mama, so he won't hurt nobody. I fix him pint by pint.

MRS. DEWEY. It's great, baby.

MATEO. I seen him when he's ugly, and truly, Mama, he's unforgivable, but somehow, my heart forgives him. Pint by pint.

MRS. DEWEY. I wish I could do the same, Chelsea.

MATEO. Try, Mama. You have to try. Or else my death's for nothin'.

*(***MATEO*** lays his hand gently on her head.)*

MRS. DEWEY. Dear Jesus.

MATEO. Whatever befalls him, befalls me. Sinking now. My words falling back in the mouth of this pitiful man. I'm not hardly a whisper, Mama.

MRS. DEWEY. Baby…

MATEO. Not hardly a murmur…

*(***MATEO*** grips his chest and staggers.)*

MRS. DEWEY. Chelsea?

MATEO. *(in his own gruff voice)* What you lookin' at? Spare me your pity.

(He grabs the duffel bag and rushes out.)

MRS. DEWEY. Chelsea, baby? Chelsea….

*(***MRS. DEWEY*** goes to her altar and closes it. She signs through her tears the first strains of a new song as she follows* **MATEO** *out.)*

MRS. DEWEY. Walk in the light…the beautiful light…

(Lights up on **LEE** *lying on the ground, asleep.* **AMA** *enters and places a cup of soup by him.* **LEE** *stirs with a groan.)*

LEE. How long have I been out?

AMA. A few hours. I brought you some *caldito.* Go back to sleep if you want. I can reheat it.

LEE. *Gracias.* I'll take it. Is there some water?

AMA. Here.

*(***AMA** *pours him a glass.)*

LEE. This smells good. *Es…lengua?*

(She shakes her head. **LEE** *drinks the water down.)*

AMA. You better eat. You look pale.

LEE. *Gracias, señora.*

AMA. I used to make that soup for Mateo when he would come home from those long nights out. Drunk and sad. Face like a closed book. Only sixteen and so lonely.

LEE. You still see him that way, don't you?

AMA. He's my boy. Whatever happens, this fact does not change. The world can detest him, God can forsake him but his *Ama* never leaves his side.

LEE. You don't believe him anymore.

AMA. We all have our *desgracias.* Our shames. When yours are revealed and you're called to Judgment, better pray your mother has a broom.

LEE. Well said. Can I quote you?

AMA. Yes, Mr. Rosenblum. You can quote me. What are you doing in this business anyway? Do you like this work?

LEE. I wanted to be a writer. But I guess I just wasn't any good at putting down my stories. So I took a job telling other people's stories. I just never figured they would resemble my own.

AMA. You mean this story?

LEE. Your life here, this house, its flaking paint. The way mimosa trees bloom in the summer, the smell of my mother's cooking. It all used to be mine. Except this old figurine. What does it represent?

AMA. *Xipe Totec.* His father brought it a long time ago. Our Lord the Flayed One. A god of renewal.

LEE. Is that a mask he's wearing?

AMA. The skin of his victim. After a sacrifice, the Aztec priest put on the flayed skin of his "volunteer" and became the God. Seeing through the eyeholes of death, one appreciates life in a terrible new way.

LEE. I guess that's true.

AMA. Tell me about your mother. *¿Era buena gente?*

LEE. Yes. She was good people. But she always seemed a little inside herself. I think she married my stepfather, a Jew who never left Manhattan, to help her forget, to get away from what we had here.

AMA. What did you need to get away from?

LEE. *(shrugs)* All I know is the yearning never goes away.

AMA. Where is your real father?

LEE. Somewhere in here, I carry the best and worst of him. The best I'm oblivious to. It's the worst I keep holding on to.

AMA. Then that's what you'll remember.

LEE. I guess we all have our Belen.

AMA. Belen? What do you mean?

LEE. Well…I guess sooner or later you'll know…

AMA. Know what?

LEE. About Mateo's half-sister. By your husband. He had another family in Mexico.

AMA. That's not true.

LEE. He said he tracked his father down to Belen, a small village where he met his sister.

AMA. Belen? Belen is the name of the junior high school he went to.

LEE. Hold on…

AMA. His father never went to Mexico. He hated it. He'd go for weeks to the racetrack in Albuquerque and get drunk there, but never Mexico. If he went, they'd never let him back across. He was an illegal.

LEE. But he said he met Sonia –

AMA. Sonia? Who's that? What has Mateo been telling you?

LEE. Where is he?

AMA. He's out.

LEE. Out? Where out?

AMA. He went out the back way. He said he was going to pick up some pictures.

LEE. WHAT?

AMA. What have you been listening to?

LEE. Oh my God. Oh my God.

*(**LEE** runs out, with **AMA** close behind. The motel room. **DRU** is packing her things. Her photographs lay displayed all over the bed. **MATEO** pushes the maid's cleaning cart in, the duffel bag resting atop it.)*

MATEO. *¿Permiso entrar, señorita?*

DRU. What are you doing here?

MATEO. This room looks kinda familiar.

*(**DRU** tries to escape but he shuts off her route with the cart.)*

MATEO. This where you and him been sleepin'?

DRU. What do you want?

MATEO. Well, first. I have a burning question on my mind only you can answer.

DRU. What's that?

MATEO. What the hell's an F-stop?

DRU. It's an aperture setting. For determining how much light gets through. And how much of the image stays in darkness. Something like that.

MATEO. Hm. I wanna apologize for hurting you the other day. I'm not keen on all them photographic lights. Oh, you got them already. Can I see?

(He scrupulously scans the array of shots.)

Looka that. Damn. You know, I don't take too many pictures 'cause I'm vain and I tend to come unglued when I see bad ones of me showed around. So it's a fortunate thing that you're so good. You gotta eye for detail.

DRU. Get out.

MATEO. Which one do you like best?

DRU. I don't like any of them.

MATEO. But which one captures my essence? Your boyfriend says you're tops at doing that.

DRU. None of them. They're no good. I'm no good. I'm quitting this job.

MATEO. Too bad. I kinda fancy them. I look kinda smart in that one.

DRU. Maybe you are. Where's Rosenblum?

MATEO. Rosenblum's dead. Leandro Guerra is resting up at my house. He's been working real hard. Digging into territory he don't know much about. Him and that little recorder. Have you known him long?

DRU. What's it to you?

MATEO. Do you love him?

DRU. Get the fuck out of my room, Mr. Buenaventura.

MATEO. DO YOU LOVE HIM.

DRU. WHAT'S IT TO YOU? WHY SHOULD I TELL YOU ANYTHING?

MATEO. Then don't.

DRU. What does this Leandro person have to do with Lee?

MATEO. He hasn't told you? Thass his real name. Leandro. He's a Mexican down to his roots. I helped him come to terms with his culture. He been lying to you?

DRU. We don't lie.

MATEO. Oh, we're all in the business of falsehood, Miss Dru. So much deceit, the lies are like pollen, all over the air, landing in people's mouths, generatin' theirselves everywhere. See? All these Mateo Buenaventuras on your bed, all of them lies ready to take to the air. People will see this and believe it.

DRU. What the hell do you want?

MATEO. If you love him, you'll give me all your pictures, the negatives, too, and get him out of here. Go back to New York. Print another lie. Not this one.

DRU. Are you serious?

MATEO. I don't want these pictures out.

DRU. What about your vanity?

MATEO. Don't give me no guff. Life's too short for guff.

DRU. What if I don't let you have them?

(He takes the cutting shear out of the bag and admires its lethal edges.)

MATEO. Draw your own conclusions, bitch. I'd just as soon leave here with your eye for detail in my pocket than without. But I'm leaving with the pictures.

DRU. I'm not afraid of you. You can't hurt me. You're the chickenshit here.

*(**MATEO** draws himself inward for a moment. Then he moves toward her with the shears.)*

MATEO. Only in the madness of our dreams do we get this chance. Only when the waste of years is washed down with Turkey and Coke and our hand jerks away at some imitation of love, do we make such goddamn fools of ourselves. But sometimes we roll a seven. Get a second chance. Make up for the past. For lapses in judgment. And love.

DRU. Love?

MATEO. The creases in my heart these last twelve years have been caulked with blood cum tears and rot. A woman like you would heal what needs healin'.

(He almost slips his hand inside her blouse, over her heart. **DRU** *quickly slides out from beneath him and darts to the photos and negatives and takes them to the maid's cart, where she dumps them into a bucket and pours floor cleaner into it.)*

MATEO. The tapes.

*(***DRU** *gets the tapes from* **LEE***'s computer bag and gives them to him.)*

MATEO. And that computer?

DRU. Not a single word in there about you. But don't believe me. Take it if you want.

MATEO. *Señorita* Dru, forgive me for hurting you. You gotta realize I'm as flawed as the next man.

DRU. You don't fool me. I've seen you butchers before. You're all the same. You think you win, you think you're entitled to be predators, in your sick heads you expect someone will say the magic word and make everything swell. Well, not me. You don't know shit about forgiveness. You don't understand mercy. Or else you would have shown some to Shannon Trimble. It's just all a convenient excuse for you. You're right, these pictures, they're all lies.

(She reaches in her pocket for a set of dog-eared snapshots.)

These you took after you clamped your paws on my throat. It's me. Like I've never seen myself. Scared shitless. Like I'm going to die. This is as close as we get to evil. Because it's in what you do! It's in the pain you make! These pictures I'm keeping.

*(***MATEO** *glowers darkly and starts toward her.* **LEE** *calls from a distance.)*

LEE. *(off)* Dru! Dru!

MATEO. Ask him about his sister. Ask him to introduce you to Sonia.

*(***LEE** *bursts into the room.)*

LEE. Mateo, stand back! Stand your ass back! Okay. What's happened?

MATEO. Nothing's happened.

*(**MATEO** leaves.)*

LEE. Dru? Are you all right?

DRU. I'm through. I'm going home.

LEE. Wait, wait. What did he come for? Where are the pictures?

DRU. They're in there. Help yourself.

LEE. What the hell? Did he do this?

DRU. I did it.

LEE. You? Are you out of your mind?

DRU. I'll save you a seat on the plane, Lee. I'm out.

LEE. You ruined them! You fucking ruined them! Jesus Christ!

DRU. You should do the same with your story.

LEE. What did he tell you? What did he say?

DRU. Those interviews are shit, Lee. You can't use them. He's a liar.

LEE. I don't believe this. What do you mean I can't use them? Where's my tapes?

DRU. I'm going.

LEE. Where are my tapes?

DRU. Who cares anymore –

LEE. WHERE ARE MY TAPES!

DRU. THEY'RE GONE, LEE! THE TAPES, THE PICTURES, THE STORY, ALL GONE! HE'S GOT THEM!

LEE. ARE YOU CRAZY! WHAT HAVE YOU DONE!

DRU. THEY'RE LIES! NOTHING BUT SICK LIES! THAT MAN FED YOU GRADE A BULLSHIT AND YOU FELL FOR IT!

LEE. IT'S NOT BULLSHIT! THIS IS MY STORY! THIS IS MY LIFE, DRU!

DRU. Tell me, baby. Are you Leandro? He says that's who you really are. Is that true?

LEE. That fuck.

DRU. Lee, is that really who you are?

LEE. He's a liar.

DRU. And who is Sonia?

LEE. Sonia?

DRU. He said to ask you. Something about your sister. But you don't have a sister, do you?

LEE. My sister?

DRU. What's going on? What've you told this animal?

LEE. Oh no. Oh no.

DRU. Who is this sister, Lee? Who is Sonia? What do these names have to do with the tapes? Why didn't you mention any of this before?

LEE. They're all lies. LIES, DRU! FUCKING LIES LIES LIES LIES LIES!

(He throws her on the bed and commences strangling her.)

DRU. LEE! STOP! STOP!

(He chokes her until she is still. Lights change. **LEE** *feels himself in the interstice. The terrible power.* **MATEO** *appears in his patio. He mutters the parenthetical text.)*

LEE/(MATEO). Prima facie
in the evidence rendered
the time recovered, (**time unfelt**)
in the corroboration of events, (**the witness statements**)
I begin to see her (**begin to put together**)
the victimology (**pristine**) undisturbed, (**uncorrupted**) hardly even here, I am hardly even here, primae facie bears me out, I'm not even here, (**I'm gone**) dissolved like emulsion (**no evidence**) no time recovered (**nothing corroborated**)

*(***LEE** *picks up the bag of tools and turns to* **MATEO***.)*

LEE. Belen. Belen Jr. High. You never had a sister. Or did you? Are you going to say something?

There's no Belen. No Sonia. No pictures. No interviews. No Evil.

What have you made me do, Mateo?

MATEO. I made you remember. It only seemed like my life.

LEE. But you said Sonia – .

MATEO. I never said Sonia. You did. She's your sister, ain't she?

LEE. Oh my god.

*(**LEE** starts to retch. Awful dry heaves.)*

MATEO. You gave me the details and I put them in my soup. Your sis and the rose embroidery on her pillow. Your old man and his bullring walk. The nights you watched over her. The fearsomeness of Mexico. All in your *Sopa de Lengua.* It's your story.

LEE. Oh my god.

MATEO. How your daddy had his way with you but left her alone. How you slipped into your baby sister's bed out of a perverted sense of pertection and then of punishment. How you lost her, anyhoo, when your old man took her away. Brother, you can disown the memory. But it's the memory that owns you.

LEE. Then Belen –

MATEO. – is real if you want it. It's a dirt town in Mexico and it's a little girl's bedroom in Fabens. A border that's both a river and a dark hallway you gotta cross for her. There's only one Sonia, and, buddy, she was yours, but you know what? She's mine now. I own your story like I own her, in this heart, *para siempre.*

LEE. Oh god.

MATEO. See, I learned psychology at that hospital. I picked you like you picked me. It was stamped into your face. This is a lover of sisters. A lover of death.

LEE. No.

MATEO. But damn. I'm starting to wonder if your old man diddled you at all. Maybe that's somethin' you perjected on him to keep from facing up to your filth. *Alomejor* he took her to Mexico to get her away from **you**!

LEE. STOP IT!

MATEO. Now you know something about evil. Now you know Leandro Guerra. You still don't know jack about me, though. Never.

So…is she dead? Did you carve up your sweet Dru?

(**LEE** *gathers himself and stands.)*

LEE. You want me to tell you? *¿Quieres ver lo que pasó?*

(The lights change as **LEE** *reenacts* **MATEO**'s *crime.)*

LEE. In a bar. Out by Midland. I sit there drinking, remembering, stewing, quietly feeling the same old dirty things with this new heart of mine. Then two people come in. Barry Stokes…And Shannon Trimble.

(**SHANNON**, *tipsy, enters and stands in the spotlight.)*

Look at her. Look at her!

(**MATEO** *does.* **LEE** *shouts for her.)*

SHANNON!!

SHANNON. Over here! No need to bellow at me!

LEE. They dance. I watch them dance.

(**SHANNON** *dances with her arms around the space her boyfriend fills.)*

LEE. I see that big burly man twice that girl's age kissing on her neck and her ear and put his hand on her ass and maybe even try to slip it up her skirt….

SHANNON. Quit! I said, quit!

LEE. And that calls some darkness up. Rage, betrayal, the resentment of years before. Something goes off in that cerebral annex I call a dick.

SHANNON. Quit, I said! Barry, take me home!

LEE. We just got here!

SHANNON. Take me home now! Dammit!

LEE. *(as* **BARRY***)* Don't pitch a fit on me here, girl! I'll slap you upside the head!

SHANNON. That's it! Home!

*(***SHANNON** *breaks away and staggers in a new space.)*

LEE. So when they go, it's a relief. Seeing those big hands all over her pale young skin. Who knows what I feel now. Last Call! But I stay awhile and drink some more and finally off I go. Back to that skanky room I call home. And I'm driving. And I see her. Just as I'm fiddling with my radio. I Fall to Pieces.

SHANNON. How about a lift home, mister?

LEE. And she's in beside you. Smell of beer and Estee Lauder.

*(***SHANNON** *stands beside* **LEE***.)*

I'm not even thinking now. Not an evil thought in my head. But something is stirring. Something I haven't felt good about in years. So I tell her I got some high-class dope in my room and would she like to smoke it. And she says –

SHANNON. Sure.

LEE. So I take her there.

(They go to the motel room. **MATEO** *watches from his seat in the patio.)*

SHANNON. So this is your party palace!

LEE. I tell her to make herself comfy.

SHANNON. Honey, I'm always comfy. But I need to pee.

LEE. Right in there.

SHANNON. And as she sashays across the room to the toilet, you watch her move in slow motion, you take in every sway of her hips, every lilt of her youthful head, the bounce of lissome high school hair beckoning life and joy and ruinous abandon.

LEE. I am getting laid tonight.

SHANNON. Get your rolling papers, Pancho!

(**SHANNON** *starts to go but stops with her back turned.)*

LEE. Suddenly, with her absence I start to feel Absence, desire bereft of body –

MATEO. – this ain't what happened.

LEE. This is **my** story now.

MATEO. I wasn't there.

LEE. I AM! I am sitting in your skin feeling this crazy numbness strangle me. Then I know. I understand. Right there. In the interstice, right on the fucking f-stop. What you need is Sonia. But there is no Sonia. There never was any Sonia in your life to show you love, no matter how depraved. You don't know how to love, Mateo. You don't know how to feel. This numbness you only know as Belen, that's what you are. Not even this new transplanted heart can make you feel love.

SHANNON. I'll be right out, mister!

LEE. But maybe hers can. So I break the glass inside my legs and go to the door and open it and go to my truck and reach in the bed for my toolbox and I lift it and carry it back to the room.

(He drops the bag of tools on the floor.)

And here's what I overlooked. What you refused to see. The victimology. Her story.

(**SHANNON** *turns and stands poised between* **MATEO** *and* **LEE**.*)*

SHANNON. Unaware of the change in the man, I come back.

LEE. The girl from the bar.

SHANNON. Eager to get stoned.

LEE. Shannon Trimble.

SHANNON. I wanna get stoned.

LEE. Standing in the accident of time.

SHANNON. I wanna get stoned now!

LEE. Prima facie.

SHANNON. And I look around. No papers, no dope, no nothin'. Only an old Messican fool with this beatific look on his face and a toolbox at his feet.

LEE. I am hardly even here.

*(***LEE** *plays out the instructions* **SHANNON** *gives over the still body of* **DRU***.)*

SHANNON. First he comes to me and kisses me on the lips. Like so, like he's short of breath and I let him.

LEE. I am hardly even here.

SHANNON. Then his hands rise up to my throat and start to press upon it. Then I get scared and I don't let him.

LEE. I am hardly even here.

SHANNON. I kick this way and that but he only tightens his grip and I scream but the scream frays where it meets the air and I know I am going to die.

LEE. Hardly even here.

SHANNON. I cry for my mother and my father and then for Barry that son of a bitch and terror like nothing I have ever felt before fills my brain and it crashes and I pass out and then die I die I am dead all my senses locked in this cold unfair unwished-for iron-wrought death.

LEE. I am hardly even here.

SHANNON. He places me gently on the carpet like a suit he just bought.

LEE. I am hardly even here.

SHANNON. He strokes the bruise petals on my neck, the little black roses of death.

LEE. I am hardly even here.

SHANNON. Then he turns to his toolbox. Oh, how I wish I had the breath to curse you.

*(***LEE** *goes to the bag. He takes out the shears, the hatchet, the boxcutter.)*

SHANNON. He brings them to my body and lays them down. Then my hands are placed above me, fingers reaching out like rays of light.

LEE. *(straddling the body of* **DRU***)* No more a whore, no more.

SHANNON. According to his own inscrutable cause.

LEE. I am hardly even here.

SHANNON. He undoes my blouse and regards my tits in their dead calm.

LEE. I am hardly even here.

SHANNON. Then he takes the boxcutter and cuts along a seam down my throat to my chest.

LEE. *(painfully etching a seam in the air)* My bouquet, my roses.

SHANNON. The oozing blood comes warm and consolating to his hands. Then the hatchet arches up and –

*(**LEE** takes the axe and swings it upward. The disembodied sound of a deafening WHACK.)*

SHANNON. – he thrusts into my chest the edge, jabs it hard, then again – *(Swings it down past **DRU**. Another WHACK.)* – putting all his body weight into my breastbone until it cracks the seal of bodily containment and out comes more blood and fluid.

LEE. The body guiding my hand, leading me in.

SHANNON. He takes the cutting shears and crunches through skin, bone, cartilage, and time and opens up the vault where all my feelings all my memories and tastes and aims and dreams and songs and fears and secrets all come steaming out right into his face.

LEE. *(the shears in his hand carving out the space before him)* I am hardly even here.

SHANNON. I WAS ALIVE, MOTHERFUCKER! I WAS MY PARENTS' PRIDE!

He gingerly slips the boxcutter into the fruitbowl of organs and cuts away the membranes and aortic gung, and with his other hand plucks off my heart and brings it up for air, which it vainly tries to pump.

LEE. Hardly even here.

SHANNON. More his than mine now, the heart sits in his hands and he almost cries for joy. The kinda joy I never expressed but at pep rallies.

LEE. *Mio.*

SHANNON. He holds it in his hands like the catch of the day and sees himself reflected in the teeming gore. Something, a mystery, a miracle of evil, makes my heart vanish from the earth and NOW he is free to love.

LEE. I am hardly even here.

SHANNON. He undoes his pants raises my skirt and pulls my legs up to him.

MATEO/LEE. Hardly even here.

SHANNON. And he enters.

MATEO. Hardly.

SHANNON. Not the body of Shannon Trimble who is gone forever now, not the girl who almost signed up for Cosmetology College this summer.

MATEO. Hardly even here.

SHANNON. He enters another time, a faraway place, an altar, full of strange faces and languages –

MATEO. Hardly even here.

SHANNON. He enters the body of a young girl, a shadow of himself, a love denied –

MATEO. Hardly even here.

SHANNON. And he feels the release of all his shame the heat the searing youth return he feels good –

MATEO. Hardly.

SHANNON. He feels good –

MATEO. Hardly.

SHANNON. He feels so good!

MATEO. Hardly!

LEE. PAPAAA!

SHANNON. Till he dissolves in his own cleansing, in his own fluids, in the acid of pure memory, Mateo Buenaventura is hardly even here.

MATEO. Not even here.

SHANNON. He sees with mounting sadness the torso of his love opened like a flower and buttoning himself up, gathering his strength, he takes my body up and places it on the bed. But my body is not Peace.
IT IS ALL OPEN ANGER.

*(**SHANNON** steps off into the darkness.)*

LEE. The tools go in the toolbox and the toolbox goes in some canyon and I go back to the day-to-day. Standing naked, in the man-made lake off the road, dazed, bedraggled, but somehow spared.

*(He stands before **MATEO**, both of them caught, accused, angry.)*

LEE. Prima facie. Your own black eden. Darkest Belen. Our Belen.

MATEO. *Chingao.*

LEE. You killed her. Do you see that now? Do you see what you are?

MATEO. I see.

LEE. But the heart, the girl's heart, I thought I had it. But I lost it. I lost it.

MATEO. You know where it is. It's with Sonia. Waiting.

LEE. You twisted old man.

MATEO. Finish the story, Leandro. I ain't scared. Are you?

*(**MATEO** takes up the bag of tools and they walk off together. **MRS. DEWEY** enters singing with a renewed hope in he voice.)*

MRS. DEWEY. Walk in the light, the beautiful light, walk in the light with Jesus beside....

(She sets up her shrine before the house as in the beginning.)

MRS. DEWEY. *Bendito* be my God. *Bendito* to forgive. *Bendito* a world where even the sweetest good can live on in the darkest soul. Mateo, I release you so that I may lay my child to rest.

(In the motel, **DRU** *suddenly awakens, coughing and gagging on the bed.)*

DRU. Lee. Lee. You can't believe him. Please don't believe him…Lee….

(She passes out. **MRS. DEWEY** *kisses the picture of her Chelsea and seals it in the suitcase.)*

MRS. DEWEY. *Bendito.*

(A cry. **AMA** *bursts forth in a frenzy.)*

AMA. *¡AAAYYYY! ¡AYYY! ¡SANGRE EN MI CASA! ¡SANGRE!*

MRS. DEWEY. What is it? Oh God. What's happened?

AMA. *¡AY, HIJO MIO! ¡HIJO MIO, QUE HORROR!*

MRS. DEWEY. Has he killed again? Has Mateo killed again?

AMA. NO! NOOO! MY BOY SLAUGHTERED! HE'S BEEN MURDERED! *¡ASESINO!*

*(***LEE** *enters, soaked in blood, carrying a white paper bag, shivering madly.* **AMA** *flees in terror.)*

AMA. *¡EL DEMONIO! ¡AGGGHH!*

MRS. DEWEY. Oh Lord.

LEE. Mrs. Dewey.

MRS. DEWEY. You poor man. What have you done? Oh my heavens.

LEE. I've been there, Mrs. Dewey. I've gone down to that darkness and sought the wicked out.

MRS. DEWEY. I told you to get away! I told you nothing good would come of this!

LEE. I have stood where killers stood and put my hand on death.

MRS. DEWEY. Curse the day! Curse the day, O Lord!

LEE. Rejoice, ma'am. God's on the cover again.

MRS. DEWEY. I don't know what you mean.

LEE. Balance. We're all trying to find balance. How do we get back to Belen?

MRS. DEWEY. We pray.

LEE. We could do that too. Anyway, your prayers have come to pass.

*(**LEE** offers her the white paper sack. The swelling red stain of blood weighs it down.)*

LEE. He fought me hard for it. But I got it for you.

MRS. DEWEY. *(backing away in horror)* Oh. God. Dear. God. This is not how, Lee.

LEE. Here, Mrs. Dewey.

MRS. DEWEY. You poor man. Now you are bride to his darkness. God have mercy.

(She goes.)

LEE. As in the beginning, so in the end. Standing on the cusp, past and past, the same bag, the ending of the story in the bag.

*(**SONIA**, wearing her white dress, enters with her bundle. She sits and arrays the pretty cotton dresses on the ground like fanning beds of flowers. Stricken, hollowed, but strangely heartened, **LEE** watches her.)*

SONIA. Right about now all the *turistas* come out of the *mesones* into the square. Ready to buy their colorful curios to take back across.

LEE. Mercy, sweet mercy in pima. Sonia.

SONIA. You see any *turistas*?

LEE. Forgive me, Sonia, I never meant –

SONIA. Do you?

LEE. No. *No turistas.*

SONIA. *Ama y yo*, we sew them in our house. The fabric comes from Jalisco but the embroidery is all ours. The lace here. I did that.

LEE. Beautiful.

SONIA. All by hand. Those little purple roses are not easy. *¿Como te llamas?*

LEE. *Leandro.*

(**SONIA** *gazes innocently at him and smiles.* **DRU** *in the motel room, rousing herself from the bed, watches piteously the scene between them.)*

SONIA. *Leandro.*

LEE. And in her smile, the pity, the shame, the obligations of blood and time vanish, oh, for that look you give me, oh, for that tenderness, Sonia, *mi amorosa, mi hermana,* for that touch I would die, I would give this heart to you, I would turn it into sweet bread for you, I would carry you away to that sacred home, that hive of all desire, that creche of baby satan, Belen. Belen. Belen.

(**LEE** *stands over* **SONIA**, *each in their bliss, as* **DRU** *weeps for them.)*

(Lights fade to blackout.)

End of Play

Also by
Octavio Solis...

Dreamlandia

Lydia

Breinigsville, PA USA
09 January 2011
252887BV00005B/3/P